7788x2

SEEK AND DESTROY

The man behind the desk told Carradine about intelligence reports of the Reds secretly building launching sites for intercontinental ballistic missiles in South America, obviously hoping to force a shift of military power against NATO. The nuclear warheads for these missiles were on their way from Russia and Carradine's job was to prevent them from reaching their destination — wherever that may be . . . But a trap had already been laid for Carradine — cunningly baited with a beautiful girl called Valentina . . .

MANNING K. ROBERTSON

SEEK AND DESTROY

Complete and Unabridged

LINFORD
Leicester

First published in Great Britain in 1965

First Linford Edition
published 2005

British Library CIP Data

Robertson, Manning K.
   Seek and destroy.—Large print ed.—
Linford mystery library
   1. Arms transfers—Soviet Union—Fiction
   2. Nuclear weapons—Fiction
   3. Cold War—Fiction
   4. Suspense fiction 5. Large type books
   I. Title
   823.9′14 [F]

   ISBN 1–84395–824–4

Published by
F. A. Thorpe (Publishing)
Anstey, Leicestershire

Set by Words & Graphics Ltd.
Anstey, Leicestershire
Printed and bound in Great Britain by
T. J. International Ltd., Padstow, Cornwall

This book is printed on acid-free paper

1

The Agents of Fear

The house stood alone. On either side of it, and behind it, was the great area of the city. The two possessed a certain affinity; an air of well-being, of peace and suburban serenity. Even though it was situated on the outskirts of Montevideo in the Treinta y Tres, the house had been subtly altered over the past eighteen years, so that now it had a Gothic air about it, a way of remembering the past for the man who lived there.

His real name was Gunther Henkel; but for the past eighteen years it had been Carlos de Silva, a man of independent means, extremely wealthy, and of a curiously retiring nature, seldom seen in the city, living with his daughter and a single manservant. He was a forgotten man, forgotten since the end of the war which had ravaged the whole of Europe, since the perpetrator-in-chief had died in a brief blaze of petrol fire with his mistress Eva Braun.

It was because of his pre-war work on high-altitude rockets that he came to the notice of Reichmarshal Goering and he was uprooted from his studies at Zurich and transferred under conditions of top security to one of the secret rocket establishments fifty miles from Berlin. The transfer could not have suited Henkel better. The work at the University had been hampered by lack of funds. Now, for the first time in his career, funds were unlimited. The work had the direct approval of the Feuhrer himself.

Seven months after the Allied invasion of Europe, and following the failure of the V1 and V2 rockets to turn the tide of war in Germany's favour Henkel realized that the course of the war had already been decided, that the Third Reich was finished, and as one of the topmost rocket experts in Germany, his own position after the war could be an extremely precarious one.

Accordingly, he had secretly and

carefully changed all of his wealth into diamonds and when the war ended, he had been ready. Like many others, his plans had been laid well. It had been difficult to obtain diamonds in Germany during the last few months of the war; it had been almost ridiculously easy to get out of Europe with his daughter Gerda, on to the ship which had brought him to Uraguay. By the time he had sold most of the diamonds, to dealers who asked no questions as to their origin, he had sufficient money to ensure a life of ease and comfort

Now, eighteen years later, Henkel, staring out of the window of the house, looking down on to the wide, spacious grounds, gleaming faintly in the glow of moonlight, smiled contentedly at his own reflection in the clear glass.

From the outside, the house had its atmosphere of peace and quiet and serenity, from the single lighted window on the ground floor, to the shadowed gables, dark against the night sky. But the quiet and the serenity were false.

The light from the window brought its

own shadows. It touched the outer fringes of the bushes but left the rest of them in darkness.

Half an hour earlier a car had purred into the plaza some twenty yards from the entrance of the grounds. With the engine switched off and the interior in darkness, it sat unnoticed, well away from the nearest lamp, in the pool of shadow thrown by the tall trees. The man seated behind the wheel checked the watch on his left wrist. It was the first movement either of the two men in the car had made for ten minutes.

Vslevov, seated beside him, gave a quick glance. It was almost time. Inwardly he was glad that on this occasion their orders were to take this man alive. He was sick of murder. For the past eight months he had enjoyed his stay in this country, so different from the bitter cold of Russia. It was part of his work to kill, to destroy. He did not enjoy doing it, he scarcely ever had, but there were occasions when it had to be done and he did it efficiently and without trying to think too much about it.

4

Kronovitch now, was different in every way. Jenko Kronovitch was an exceedingly dangerous member of society, even in Russia where a great deal of killing had to be done, all justified by the need to rid the country of those who were considered to be enemies of the State. Ordinarily, he might have been put in a place where he could do no harm, but the M.G.B. were always on the lookout for men capable of carrying out orders without question, completely trustworthy.

'You are sure that he will be alone in the house?' Kronovitch did not turn his head as he spoke.

Vslevov nodded quickly. 'His daughter left two hours ago. She will not return until after midnight.'

'After midnight?' There was a slight lifting of the thick brows. 'Please be more exact, Comrade.'

Vslevov swallowed. He began to tremble a little inside. He knew it would be a waste of time to apologize. This vagueness was contrary to discipline. 'She will arrive back at the house between twelve-fifteen and twelve-thirty.'

'And the servant?'

'This is the night when he goes into the city. He will not return until morning.'

'Excellent.' Kronovitch opened the door of the car, stepped silently out, closing it behind him. Together they made their way along the wide street, keeping to the shadows thrown by the trees. Soon, on their right, barbed iron railings stretched along the street. Beyond them, half-hidden behind the trees stood the well-proportioned brick house with its Gothic gables, all in darkness except for the window on the ground floor. Kronovitch glanced up, almost idly, noticing the rolls of barbed wire which ran along the top of the railings. Obviously Henkel had taken certain precautions in spite of the fact that he probably believed himself secure here, hiding behind the new name, the new life, he had made for himself.

The tall gates were securely locked. There was possibly some hidden warning system fitted to them anyway. Thirty yards further on the railings merged with a high stone wall and it was here that he found what he had been looking for. The gap in the railings was wider at this point, wide enough for them to ease their bodies through. Warily, they moved through the trees towards the house. There was an open courtyard in front of the house. Vslevov moved out into the open, bit down on the gasp of pain as Kronovitch's hand closed about his upper arm in a grip of steel. Two shadows padded across a patch of moonlight, stood for a moment with their massive heads lifted to the sky as if scenting the presence of the two men among the trees. A moment later they came forward at a swift lope, lips drawn back over the snarling fangs.

There was the padding of feet on the smooth concrete. Then Kronovitch had taken the tiny weapon from his pocket. Smaller than a normal gun, it seemed dwarfed by his ham-like fist. The dogs were less than twenty feet away when he pressed the trigger. There was scarcely any sound but the two tiny darts had each found its mark, each tipped with sufficient curare to kill a score of dogs.

Kronovitch scarcely paused to give the two bodies a second glance as he stepped

7

over them. Keeping to one side of the wide swathe of light that spilled from the downstairs window, they reached the bushes growing close to the wall of the house. Henkel would be expecting nothing. After all, eighteen years had gone by since he had escaped from Germany, carrying in his head much vital information regarding the science of rocketry. By now, thought Kronovitch grimly, much of that information must surely be out of date. But the orders direct from M.G.B. Headquarters in Moscow had been explicit and he was in no position to question the reason behind them.

The french windows were open; another sign that Henkel relied on the defences he had set up in the grounds. Vslevov switched on his torch at a signal from Kronovitch and stepped through the windows, going carefully into the room beyond. The light of the torch showed exquisite furniture, a Persian carpet, and paintings around the walls which even he recognized as original masters. Silently, the two men moved towards the door on the far side of the room. It opened noiselessly. There was a faint light in the corridor, coming from the strip of yellow that showed beneath a door halfway along it. Vslevov nodded and the other man motioned him forward.

Pausing for a moment outside the door, Kronovitch listened intently. When he heard nothing, he closed his fingers gently around the handle of the door, twisted silently. In the steady, singing silence, a small noise came from inside the room. The sound a man might make as he shifted his body into a more comfortable position in his chair. Kronovitch gave a quick nod, pushed hard at the door, forcing it open and in the same movement, he was inside the room, eyes slitted against the harsh glare of the lights.

The man seated at the desk in the middle of the room looked up sharply, the eyes behind the steel-rimmed bifocals widening in stunned surprise. Almost automatically his right arm cut across his body, swivelling in his chair.

'Stop!' called Kronovitch sharply, his voice cutting like the lash of a whip across the stillness, 'or I shall be forced to kill you.'

The other's hand had not travelled far. Now it stopped, as if frozen, a couple of inches from his pocket. 'Who are you? How did you get in here and what do you want with me?'

'You are to come with us,' Kronovitch said softly. His voice was uninterested in the other, or in any threat of the other. At the moment Henkel did not exist for him except possibly as a target if he did not do as he was told.

'Where?' For a moment there was the beginning of fear showing through on the other's face, a faint sheen of perspiration, glistening in the light. It was the reaction of a man who was beginning to guess that fate, the fate from which he had been hiding these past eighteen years, was now catching up with him.

'You will discover that soon enough, Herr Henkel.'

'Henkel? But my name is de Silva. Carlos de Silva. I have papers to prove — '

'Papers can be forged and will prove

nothing. Your name, your record, everything about you is known to us.' While he had been speaking, Vslevov had moved around to the back of the other's chair. Reaching into the other's pocket, he took out the gun and thrust it into his own. Almost automatically, Henkel swung round. Fear seemed to have given him a reckless courage which he would otherwise never have possessed. Vslevov's stiffened right hand travelled less than six inches, fingers spread out for rigidity, but the blow sent Henkel's head jerking back on his neck, his body sliding from the chair. He was unconscious before he hit the floor. Bending beside the body, Vslevov felt for the pulse, glanced up at Kronovitch and nodded his head slowly.

'He is still alive,' he said tonelessly.

'Very well. Get him down to the car.'

Vslevov picked up the unconscious body, carried it out of the room, along the corridor and through the parted french windows. In all, less than three minutes had elapsed since they had entered the house. A car passed as they reached the gates. It drove on without slowing.

11

Kronovitch glanced up and down the quiet street. There was no one. Working quickly, he forced the lock on the gates, knowing that even if a warning mechanism had been rigged there, it would now be sounding its warning to an empty house.

Sliding the unconscious man into the back of the car, Vslevov got in beside Kronovitch.

Starting the car, Kronovitch said softly: 'Keep an eye on him. He may come round and give us trouble on the way.'

Vslevov took the gun he had removed from Henkel's pocket out of his own, checked carefully that it was loaded, that the safety catch was off, then settled himself back in his seat as the other let in the clutch, moving the high-powered car away from the kerb and along the deserted street.

A hundred yards along the street, a car suddenly swung around the corner, the powerful glare of the headlights sweeping over them, half-blinding Kronovitch as he pulled hard on the wheel, tyres bleating along the edge of the pavement. He swore fluently in Russian, swerving violently to avoid the oncoming vehicle. For a moment, he could see nothing, aware only that the other car had somehow scraped past him with only inches to spare. Whoever had been in that car would have seen them both clearly in that blinding light. Even though there seemed no possible way in which they could be connected with Henkel's disappearance, it was something which his tidy and meticulous mind did not like. No sooner had the other car gone past them, straightening up now that the danger was past, than Vslevov said sharply: 'The driver of that car, Comrade. Did you see who it was?'

'How did you expect me to see who was driving that car when I could not even see the road ahead of me?' snapped the other tightly. His voice was cold. 'Was it of any importance?'

'It was the girl — Henkel's daughter. I'm sure of it.'

Kronovitch's heavy face was suddenly suffused with anger. 'You are sure of this? She was not due back at the house for another hour — if your information was correct.'

'Perhaps she decided to return earlier. It has never happened before and I have watched the house for more than two months.'

Kronovitch was silent for a long moment, concentrating on the road which was leading them out of the city, into the dark country to the west of Montevideo. Then, stretching his lips back over his teeth, he spoke in short, clipped syllables, his voice coming out in a sort of sibilant hiss.

'We must assume that she saw us and that she could recognize us again. That could be extremely embarrassing, particularly if she gives our descriptions to the police.' He paused to allow time for the significance of his words to sink in. 'I shall take Henkel the rest of the way. Ten miles along the road there is a garage which is open all night. You will hire a car there, drive back into the city and take care of the girl. You understand?'

An inaudible sigh came from Vslevov's lips as he straightened abruptly in his

14

seat. His fingers tightened around the pistol. 'You want me to take her alive, keep her somewhere where she can do no harm.'

Knowing what was in the other's mind, Kronovitch paused for the barest fraction of a second, then said in his softest voice: 'Comrade. I have to tell you that this mission is one of the utmost importance as far as M.G.B. is concerned. Unless we act correctly and without hesitation, there will be trouble.' He sought for some final phrase which would express the full threat, convey the terror to his companion, without actually defining it in so many words and at last he added: 'If we fail and the girl causes trouble for us, there will be questions asked in Moscow, questions which will have to be answered here.'

'I understand,' Vslevov said tautly. As they drove swiftly into the night along a section of the road which seemed to be badly cambered, he was feeling oddly dissatisfied. Back to murder again. But he knew the rules. Sitting in the hurtling car beside Kronovitch, he felt touched by some of that strangely indefinable fear he had known first of all in Moscow when he had realized for the first time that one day he might make his first small mistake which could have the most dreadful consequences for him. He lit a cigarette and tried to see into the darkness which shrouded them on all sides, except where the headlights of the car, rising and falling in front of them, touched briefly on the surface of the road as it wound and twisted through the quiet countryside.

* * *

The car had arrived punctually on time outside the entrance of the hotel exactly three minutes earlier. The chauffeur, elegantly clad in a dark blue uniform with no distinguishing marks on the lapels, hurried forward to open the door as Steve Carradine stepped out into the street, then crossed the pavement and lowered his head as he stepped into the car, settling his long body down in the soft upholstery. At least everything was always done in style whenever he received an

16

urgent call to Headquarters. The chauffeur settled in behind the wheel, took the car away from the kerb, out into the main stream of traffic. As they drove across London, Carradine turned over in his mind the various possibilities which could have been behind the telephone call he had received the night before. He reached into his pocket for the slim cigarette case, extracted a cigarette, lit it. The pistol in the shoulder holster made a barely perceptible bulge in the expensively-cut suit. There was no outward indication of the other weapons he carried on his person. The slim, long-bladed throwing knife strapped to his wrist, not a hint of the razor-sharp blade in the heel of his right shoe. His other attributes were equally invisible, and equally deadly.

A holder of the Black Belt for Judo, an expert in the art of karate. An excellent knowledge of several languages, speaking Spanish and Russian fluently, the former due to his Spanish mother, the latter due to necessity brought about by several of his earlier missions for the British Secret Service.

Dark-haired, aged thirty-one, his appearance was that of a man who was going somewhere in an urgent haste, a good-looking face but with a hint of humour in the thin lips and wide-spaced eyes of the palest grey that seemed to look through, and never at, anyone.

The car turned off the main street, entered a narrow side-street between tall, dull houses which had been built the previous century and looked as though they had given up any attempt to regain a little of their past glory. The chauffeur handled the car skilfully between the double row of parked vehicles, brought the Rolls Royce to a gentle halt outside the tall building at the very end of the street. There was nothing about this particular building to indicate that it was any different from the score of others in the vicinity.

Inside, the place was quiet. Carradine took the elevator to the fourth floor, made his way noiselessly to the door halfway along the corridor. There was the woodpecker tapping of a typewriter in one of the other rooms, the only sound, it

18

seemed, in the whole of the building. Pausing outside the door, he rapped sharply on it, went inside as a man's voice called on him to enter, closing the door behind him.

Even though he had been inside this particular room on several occasions in the past, Carradine never failed to experience that quickening of his muscles, that faint tautness which came into his mind, almost as if there were some strange, hidden danger here which he had never been able to see. But there was nothing about the outward appearance of the room to give that impression. The simple, polished desk in one corner, arranged diagonally so that the light from the window fell slightly from behind. Three chairs, two against one wall and the third in front of the desk; five metal filing cabinets, locked and barred with a steel reinforcing rod containing Top Secret folders and, incongruously it seemed, a glass-fronted bookcase against the wall at the back of the desk.

The man seated in the chair behind the desk was chubby and balding, his face bearing an oddly cherubic expression. He gave Carradine a quick glance, then nodded towards the chair in front of his desk. Carradine sat down, waited patiently for the other to stop riffling through the sheaf of papers on the desk in front of him.

It was difficult to realize that this pleasant-looking man was the head of this, the least-known section of British Intelligence. Although he had worked with him for more than three years now, even Carradine did not know the other's name, had never seen him outside of this room.

Finally, the other looked up from the papers in front of him. Placing the tips of his fingers gently together, he said in a quiet, casual voice: 'I've got something for you, Carradine.' His lips curled into one of his frequent smiles that seemed to light up his whole countenance. 'You've no doubt been having a very easy time these past few months, but this is going to change all that quite drastically.'

Carradine gave a brisk nod. There was no need for him to answer; the other expected him to listen, only to speak if he asked a question on some point he did not understand.

'We know that the Reds have been pouring money at a fantastic rate into South America for the past two years. These — ' He tapped the pile of papers in front of him with a long forefinger, ' — are the reports of secret work that is going on down there. It seems clear that they are building launching sites for intercontinental ballistic missiles which they obviously hope to use to force a shift of military power with NATO.'

'And the nuclear warheads for these missiles, sir?' Carradine asked.

'So far as we know,' was the chilling reply, 'these have already left Russia and are on their way. Your job will be to prevent them from reaching their destination — wherever that may be.'

He paused to allow the full significance of his words to sink in, examining the face of the man in front of him.

'South America is a big place, sir.'

'Exactly. But we do have some additional information. Not much, but it may be enough for you to find something to go on.' His tone sharpened a little as he went on. 'Ever hear of a man named Gunther Henkel?'

Carradine searched his mind, then shook his head. 'I'm afraid not, sir.'

'Hmmm.' If the other was disappointed at this, he gave no other sign than the faint inflection to that single sound. He flicked the grey length of ash from the tip of his cigarette into the tray in front of him, leaned forward over the desk, resting his weight on his elbows. He went on: 'Henkel was one of the top men in the field of German rocketry during the war. I've no doubt that both the Americans and the Russians would have liked to have got their hands on him, but somehow he succeeded in slipping through their fingers, vanished utterly and without a trace. He was an extremely clever man in those days, converted everything he had into diamonds. When he got out, he had a fortune with him.'

He looked over the desk at Carradine with a mild expression. 'It took almost seventeen years for anyone to locate him.

The FBI finally traced him to Montevideo, living under an assumed name. I gather they were hoping to persuade him to go to Washington for consultations with their rocket people and then, if possible, to get him to work for them.'

'But they didn't succeed?'

'No, they didn't. Unfortunately, the Russians had not given up looking for him either. While the FBI were trying to decide on stronger measures they might employ to get him out of Uraguay, the Reds beat them to the punch. Henkel was kidnapped from Montevideo six days ago and taken to an unknown destination, but we strongly suspect that his kidnapping is linked with this other business. By now he is no doubt working for them somewhere in this area.' While he had been speaking the other had opened a drawer of his desk and taken out a map case, sliding the linen map out on to the desk and spreading it out with his fingers, putting the two heavy paperweights on two of the corners, while he motioned Carradine to hold down the others, as he made a small circle with his finger on a part of South

America which Carradine recognized as lying some five hundred miles or so to the west of Montevideo.

'I realize that's still one hell of a lot of country,' said the other mildly. 'It doesn't bring us much nearer to discovering where these launching sites are. We don't know how they got the stuff into the country in the first place. It's a certainty that little, if any, of it was manufactured in South America. It requires plenty of specialized equipment to make that sort of thing. And as for the nuclear warheads, there are possibly half a dozen ways they could get them into the country.' For the first time, the other's voice held a tired note of resignation in it. Then his eyes became sharp and commanding. 'This is going to be no easy assignment. Their agents will be watching this deal all the way. They know that the FBI were in contact with Henkel. That is possibly the reason they stepped in when they did. They'll be expecting trouble, if not from the Americans, then from us.' He smiled again, said almost angelically: 'You know, Carradine, I wouldn't be at all surprised

if they haven't already alerted some of
their top men to keep an eye open for
you. Not you personally, but whoever I
decide to put on to this job.'

★   ★   ★

The silver, ornamented clock on the wall
ticked with a maddening, incessant
sound. Normally it made only a background noise and Gerda Henkel scarcely
ever noticed it. But she had been sleeping
badly for the past six nights, her nerves
were shredded by what had happened.
Every night she had awakened during the
early hours of the morning, believing that
she heard someone moving around in the
house. Once she had got out of bed, taken
the small pistol she always carried now
from beneath her pillow, and gone down
the stairs. But there had been no one
there. Now, at last, she could stand it no
longer and had decided to leave this
place, leave the police to carry on their
investigations into the kidnapping of her
father and drive out into the country to
stay for a little while with Rosa Calleros

and her parents. She doubted if the police would get anywhere with this case. Had their organization been as effective and efficient as they claimed, they would have found something during the six days which had elapsed since that night when she had arrived home earlier than she had expected, had almost hit that car which had been travelling without lights — the car, she felt sure, which had been used to take her father away. If only she had called the police sooner when she had discovered that her father was not in the house, but there had been nothing out of the ordinary to suggest that anything was wrong. Not until she had found the two dogs lying dead in the shadows. By that time it had been too late. The kidnappers had slipped through any cordon which the police had been able to throw up around the city.

Slamming down the lid of the case, she snapped the locks, straightened up sharply as the telephone rang, loudly and insistently. Picking it up from its cradle she found herself staring at the receiver strangely. For several days she had been half-expecting to receive a call from whoever had taken her father, demanding ransom money for his safe return. The voice at the other end was unmistakably that of Inspector Santos, the Chief of Police.

'Senorita de Silva?'

'Yes, speaking.' She forced herself to control the shaking in her voice.

'I'd like you to come down to Headquarters if you would, please. There are a few further questions I would like to ask you.'

'But I've already told you everything I know three times.'

'Of course. But this will only take a few minutes. I think you should be told of new information we have received concerning your father; information which possibly has an important bearing on this case.'

'Very well. If it is so important, I'll come at once.' She replaced the receiver with trembling fingers. Leaving the suitcase on the chair, she walked to the door, turned to give a backward glance at the room, then opened the door and stepped out into the corridor. Suddenly she felt tensed and nervous. She did not know how much longer she could go on like this, not knowing anything for certain. If only she knew whether her father was dead or alive, where he was, why these people wanted him. But she knew nothing. The police, it seemed, knew very little more.

Inspector Santos sat at his desk in the roomy office of the Police Headquarters in Montevideo. Carefully, he placed the cigarette into the end of the long, slender holder, lit it, and blew a cloud of smoke into the air in front of him, spoke through the drifting blue haze.

'I deeply regret having to call you here again, Senorita,' he said, his voice smooth and silky. 'But I have recently learned something which has put this case of your father's disappearance into a very different light. Previously, I was inclined to believe that these people merely wanted money. After all, it is well known that your father is a very rich man. But then I asked myself: If that is so, why kidnap him, why not kidnap the one person who means more to him than anyone else in the world, namely yourself?' He grinned with a sly look of satisfaction.

'Do you expect me to answer that, Inspector?'

Santos shook his head very slowly. He said briefly: 'No. You see, I now know who your father really is. This name, Carlos de Silva, which he adopted years ago was the only one known to me, until one of my assistants brought me this file.' He tapped the slender folder deliberately with his forefinger.

'What is it?'

'These are the records of a man named Gunther Henkel who came to Uraguay from Germany just after the end of the war in Europe.' He saw the sudden look that passed over her face. 'I see that you understand, Senorita Henkel. Your father worked on certain secret projects for Germany during the war. When the Allies and the Russians overran your country, he decided to get out and he came here, bringing with him a not inconsiderable fortune in diamonds. He assumed the name of de Silva and in time, his past was forgotten. Now, it would appear to have caught up with him. We can never run away from fate, Senorita, no matter how hard we try.'

Gerda Henkel sat quite still in her chair. Then she shrugged her shoulders with a hint of impatience. 'Now that you know this, are you any closer to finding out where he is?'

Santos straightened abruptly in his chair. His voice cut across the table at her like a whip. 'Please remember where you are, Senorita. You are not here to ask the questions. I will do that. If I am to find your father, I shall need all of your co-operation.'

'But I have already told you everything that happened,' protested the girl. 'We've been over it three times.'

'Then if necessary, we shall go over it again.' The other's tone was deliberately hard. He picked up a pen and a pad, pulling it towards him. 'The two men you saw in the car. Describe them again to me.'

Gerda sighed. 'The man who was driving was tall, exceptionally broad in build. His face was — ' She broke off as a shudder went through her, swallowed, then continued: 'it was brutish. That is the only way to describe it. He looked like a man who would kill for the sheer pleasure of seeing another human being squirm and suffer.'

'And the other man?' So far, Santos had not written a single word on the pad in front of him. The pen was poised in his hand above the paper as if frozen there.

'He was more slightly-built, thin-faced. His head was half-turned towards me and he seemed to be holding a gun in his hand. Everything happened so quickly that it was impossible for me to make out anything more. It was all over in a few seconds. It was only because the head-lights of my car swept over them that I saw anything at all.'

'Very well, Senorita.' Santos twirled the pen in both hands. 'You can rest assured that we shall do everything in our power to find your father but in the meantime, I would suggest that you go away for a little while. I do not wish to frighten you, but I feel certain that if your father refuses to co-operate with these people, they may decide to force his hand by kidnapping you. Is there anywhere you can go for a little while?'

'I was already packing to visit some friends in the country when you rang.'

'Excellent.' Scraping back his chair, Santos got to his feet. 'I think that would be wise. But leave the address of these friends of yours with Sergeant Cordilla as you leave. It is essential that we should know where you are.'

★   ★   ★

There were many cases in Montevideo which the police had never solved. Gerda Henkel, seated behind the wheel of the car, felt sure that this would be one of them. Inspector Santos was a man who thought that he had only to assign a sufficiently large number of men to a case and it would automatically be solved in a very short time.

For a long moment she drove automatically, her eyes on the road in front of her, but her mind frozen by her thoughts.

She could not put the image of that huge man who had been seated behind the driving wheel of that darkened car out of her thoughts. She had seen his face for only that one brief moment when the headlights of her car, swinging sideways through the night as she had turned the corner, had swept over the windscreen of the other car. She realized that her hands and forearms were aching with the convulsive strength of her grip on the wheel and with a conscious mental and physical effort, forced herself to relax a little.

There was that man who had come to see her father on several occasions in the past year or so. Although she did not know for certain, she had the suspicion that he was a member of the Secret Service of one of the Western countries, either America or Britain. Should she try to get in touch with him? He was more likely to be able to help and advise her than the police in Montevideo. No, that was out of the question. She had no idea where he could be found, knew nothing about him. Desperately she cast her mind back, trying to recall anything which might help her find this man, but several moments of reflective introspection forced her to the conclusion that it was impossible. As far as she knew, he had made all of the arrangements as to times of meeting at the house, had arrived there without any warning as far as she had been concerned. If her suspicions concerning him were correct, this was what she would have expected. In a business of that sort you never made any prior arrangements, you turned up unannounced and left the same way.

A little of the fear rose up in her mind again. She tried to rid herself of it in the sheer exhilaration of speed. The road was virtually empty. Only one car, far behind her, occasionally visible in the mirror whenever she reached a long stretch of straight road. Thrusting her foot down on the accelerator, she felt the car lunge forward like an unchained animal, full of power and strength. The wheels hummed on the road. The tall mountains formed a background panorama which scarcely seemed to move, in spite of the acceleration of the car. Five miles further on the road began to twist and turn and slowly, almost reluctantly, she eased her foot from the accelerator. The speedometer, which had been reading close to ninety miles per hour, now began to slip back, the red needle falling to sixty and then fifty. She drove expertly, handling the powerful car easily.

A couple of cars passed her going in the opposite direction, and then a heavy truck trundling along at a more sedate pace. After that the road was clear again, but a quick glance in the mirror showed her that the car which had been some distance behind her had now closed up rapidly and was only a short distance behind. It was obvious that the other must have taken some of those sharp bends at high speed. Somebody in more of a hurry than she was, she thought, maintaining her speed so that the other would be able to overtake.

The other car moved up swiftly on the outside. Then it was level with her. She expected it to accelerate away now that the road was clear for several miles ahead. Instead, it remained level with her and something, some hidden instinct, prompted her to turn her head and glance momentarily at the driver of the other car. She caught only a side view of the other's profile. For several seconds, there was no feeling of danger in her mind. It took that length of time for recognition of the other to penetrate. The thin face, the flesh drawn down tightly against the cheek bones. The high-bridged nose, the lips drawn into a cruel gash of a mouth.

She felt her knees begin to tremble, tried to exert pressure on the accelerator to increase speed, to keep ahead of the other. Coldness was creeping up into her body. This was the man she had seen in the car, the man seated beside the driver. She remembered how the light had shone off the metal of the gun in his hand on that occasion, knew that she could not possibly be mistaken.

The drone of the car engine grew louder in her ears. A mile or so ahead, the road curved right in a tight bend. She must slow down now, or she would be taking that curve at a dangerously high speed. Almost of its own accord, her foot moved off the accelerator on to the brake, pressing gently on it. The car began to slow.

Too late she realized what was in the other man's mind. The other car began to drift over to her side of the road, closing the gap between them, forcing her to pull further into the side of the road. The fear in her mind, dominating every other emotion now, controlled her actions. Tyres squealed in protest on the road as she continued to apply the brakes, aware that the other meant to drive her off the road. She tried to haul hard on the wheel, to force the car back away from the edge but inexorably, the other car swung towards her.

Out of the corner of her eye she saw the fiercely-grinning face of the man in the other car. Lips were drawn back over his teeth. His eyes were wide, staring. The front bumper of the car touched the door of her own. Acting impulsively, instinctively, she spun the wheel in an attempt to slide away from him, pushing her foot down hard on the accelerator, forgetting about the curve coming up now, intent only on getting away from this madman whose sole aim seemed to be to kill her. The other car hit hers again, harder this time. It was too much for her nerves, stretched to the utmost limit. With a faint scream, she pulled on the wheel, the car slithered sharply to one side. For a moment the front wheels clawed at nothing as the ground dropped away beneath the bonnet. She had a momentary glimpse of the ground hurtling towards her, felt the rear of the car lifting high into the air as it somersaulted, then nothing . . .

2

The Bait

The change in the note of the aircraft engines wakened Carradine. Pressing the button on the side of the inclined seat, he brought it back into the upright position, twitched aside the curtain across his window and glanced out. Beyond the smooth, circular mouths of the twin jet engines, he was just able to make out the city far below them. The old section of Montevideo, he remembered, occupied the low, rocky headland which projected westwards between the estuary and the bay which formed the harbour. Newer sections of the city extended westward in the faint morning mist which lay over the ground, over a beautiful tract of country. The sea was a faint purple in the half light, fading to a dark blue, almost black out on the horizon where the sun, although still out of sight, even at this height, touched the low band of cloud with a tint of flame.

Steve Carradine glanced down at the watch on his wrist. The golden hairs on the back of his hand glistened in the faint light entering through the window. Now they were beginning to lose altitude, circling above the city which seemed no larger than a toy, laid out on some gigantic table. One by one, the other passengers were stirring, sitting up and taking stock of their surroundings. They descended into a layer of thin cloud. For a moment everything on the ground vanished from sight and there was only the white mist, holding them motionless in the air. Then, like smoke drifting past the window, the cloud thinned, the sun came bounding up above the horizon, throwing a wide swathe of red light across the sea, they were flying in over the bay and Carradine could see some of the landmarks he recalled from his last visit to this city. The Calle 18 de Julio, reckoned as one of the finest boulevards in the whole of South America, extending eastward from the Plaza de la Independencia, out to the suburbs of the city; the square towers and the large dome of the Cathedral, facing on to the Plaza de la Constitucion, perhaps the most conspicuous landmark in the entire city.

The red light flashed over the door leading into the cockpit. The man seated in front of Carradine stubbed out the cigarette he had lit only a few seconds before, fastened his safety belt across his corpulent middle and sat back in his seat. Carradine fastened his own safety belt, relaxed in his seat as the drone of the engines dropped to the faintest whisper and the thin, high-pitched shriek of the air streaming just past the plane could be clearly heard. He reflected that in spite of all that he had been told in London, he still knew very little about this affair. Launching sites for ICBMs somewhere in the wilderness far to the west of Montevideo; a man who had been one of Hitler's topmost rocket scientists disappearing without a trace a week earlier, and more ominous than anything else, the certainty — for the information gained by other agents of the Secret Service had always been disturbingly correct in the past — that the nuclear warheads for these missiles had left Russia and were on their way. How did these people hope to get them into South America? They must have given this problem a lot of thought, for it was not like the Reds to undertake anything like this unless they were absolutely positive that they could carry it through without a slip.

The buildings slid swiftly beneath the metal belly of the plane as it dropped low over the outskirts of the city. Then there was the long white strip of the runway in front of them. It seemed to have swung up into position without any warning. A bleat of rubber, protesting as it struck the ground hard, a second slight shudder, then they were down. The man in front of Carradine uttered a faintly audible sigh of relief, unfastened the belt from around his middle and thrust out his legs in front of him. Turning his head, he looked directly at Carradine, said in English: 'I always feel relieved whenever I'm on the ground again after being in one of these things.' The man was about fifty, iron-grey hair, thick-set and vigorous, the sort of man one would have expected to go to fat quickly, but somehow there was no hint of that in the other's body. He went on softly, as they taxied around the perimeter track towards the Reception Building, 'I read the statistics they publish every so often. They claim that there are fewer fatalities with flying than there are when travelling by train or car. Unfortunately, I never was one to trust in statistics. On paper, they look fine. In practice, they give me a little shiver along my spine.'

Carradine nodded. 'I know how you feel.' His voice was soft. 'Perhaps it might help if you were a fatalist like me.'

The man's thick, bushy brows lifted a little. For a moment the blue eyes watched him, seemed to penetrate all the way back to the rear of his skull, as if he were searching him with all of his senses, trying to size him up. Was there something more than a casual interest in him, showing for a brief moment at the back of the other's eyes? A look of inner calculation? He dismissed it after a moment's reflection. The plane came to a standstill. The whine of the engines climbed down from the almost inaudible shriek, moaned in their ears for a few seconds, then faded into silence.

The passage through the Customs took little time. Then Carradine was out of the tall building, his cases beside him, lifting his hand to signal to one of the waiting taxis. Out of the corner of his eye, he saw his acquaintance from the plane step out of the entrance and look up and down the wide street as if expecting someone to be there to meet him. Then Carradine's attention was directed away from the other. A black limousine purred to a standstill directly in front of him, the door was opened from inside, and the girl behind the wheel leaned forward.

'Mister Carradine?' It was more of a statement of fact than a question.

With an effort, he forced down the feeling of surprise, nodded, picked up his cases and stepped into the car, tossing the two cases into the rear seat. Was this some of Headquarters' doing, or was this something else? he wondered.

'You looked very surprised,' said the girl. She let in the clutch and the car roared away from the pavement, shot along the street, missed one of the cars in front of them by less than an inch, her left hand banging the gear lever up into third as she pressed with her foot on the accelerator pedal.

'How did you know my name, or that I would be on that plane?'

'That was quite easy. I asked to see the passenger list, saw that your name was on it and waited for you to arrive.'

'And may I ask why?'

The girl smiled, tilted her head a little to one side. There was an accent to her voice which was certainly not that of a South American. 'Let us simply say that we like to welcome visitors to our country. Do you object to me at all, Mister Carradine?'

'Steve,' said Carradine softly. He settled back in his seat as the car thundered forward along the wide highway, an angry hooting behind them sounding briefly as they shot between a car and a heavy truck lumbering in the opposite direction. Out of the corner of his eye he saw that the red needle of the speedometer was just below the hundred mark.

Her smile widened, became a trifle more provocative. 'Steve Carradine,' she said softly, her voice deep and warm. 'I like that. My name is Valentina Veronova.'

'Russian?'

'Caucasian,' corrected the girl. 'It may not seem so on the surface, but I do assure you that there is a subtle difference.'

'If you say so.' There was a pause while Carradine looked at her profile, the delicately-cut features, the clear blue eyes that were now fixed on the open road ahead of them, the finely-chiselled nose and mouth. She did not seem to mind his close scrutiny. They drove around a bend in the road, entered a straight stretch and the car leapt forward as if it had been violently kicked from behind. Carradine grinned. He said: 'Perhaps you could go a little faster if you really tried.'

'Perhaps.' The red needle crept still higher around the dial. The sides of the highway were a vaguely-seen blur as they flashed past the speeding car. He sat back calmly. If the girl was trying to scare him with this show of speed, then she was simply wasting her time. The car side-swiped violently as Valentina swung it sharply around a corner which came up on them apparently without any warning at all. Instinctively, the girl corrected, the car righted itself and they sped on along the white highway which led them towards Montevideo.

★   ★   ★

When the car with Carradine and the girl had left the Airport, the man standing near the entrance walked down towards the street, stood for a moment staring straight ahead of him, then glanced round as a car left the line of parked vehicles on the other side of the street and moved slowly towards him. Kronovitch opened the door, waited until the ther had climbed in, then pulled out into the slow-moving stream of traffic leaving the Airport.

'Were you successful?' asked Kronovitch shortly. Thoughtfully, as if this were the kernel of the entire problem, he added: 'I saw Valentina leave a few moments ago with a man. That, I presume, was Steve Carradine.'

'Da,' Chernogradtsky nodded slowly. He sat behind me on the plane. I joined the flight in London as instructed. He was never out of my sight for a single moment until he got into the car with Valentina.'

'Excellent.' Kronovitch smiled, drawing his lips back over his teeth like those of an animal scenting its prey. 'He looks a particularly nasty customer!'

Chernogradtsky's face gave the impression of mild surprise. 'He looked very little different to a great many men I saw in London,' he said.

Kronovitch shook his head. 'If you think that, Comrade, then you are making a very dangerous mistake which could be fatal as far as you are concerned unless you rectify it immediately. We know his record. It makes very interesting reading. But perhaps you have not seen it.'

'No. I was merely ordered to follow him here,' said the other stiffly.

'He is one of the most deadly of the British agents we have ever encountered. On several occasions he has thwarted our attempts to carry out our plans. We must never underestimate him. Valentina has her orders.'

'Can she be trusted?'

For a moment Kronovitch turned his head a little, taking his attention off the road in front of him, fixing the other with a hard stare. 'She is perfectly trustworthy. The M.G.B. have investigated her background thoroughly.'

'And this man, Carradine. What will happen to him?'

Kronovitch's smile took on a hard grimness. 'Steve Carradine will meet with an unfortunate accident. It will be regrettable, but unavoidable. The trap was baited in Moscow as you are no doubt aware.'

'For Carradine?'

'For whichever agent the British Secret Service chose to come out here. We know they had discovered the fact that we are building here in South America. The FBI will have informed them of Henkel's disappearance. It was anticipated that someone would be sent here. Now that we know the identity of that man, the rest should be relatively easy.'

They idled their way along the wide highway leading into Montevideo and pulled up at the end of the wide plaza. Stopping the engine, Kronovitch pointed a finger. The black car was parked outside the Hotel Uruguayo.

*   *   *

Accommodation had been arranged in advance for Carradine. In the past he had grown to rely on the efficiency of the staff at Secret Service Headquarters in London and on this occasion they had really done him proud. The hotel was certainly well up to international standards. The commissionaire and the receptionist had not raised their well-trained brows by so much as a tenth of an inch when they had caught sight of the girl who accompanied him, and as far as

Carradine was concerned, that represented the best and most reliable
indication of the standing of any hotel in
any country.

Standing at the window, Carradine
looked down into the wide, spacious
street below him. Behind him, the girl
moved forward. 'Do you like it?' she
asked in that rich voice of hers. 'They tell
me this is one of the best views of the city.
You are indeed fortunate to have this
room. Mine is across the corridor, facing
the rear of the building and — '

'You're staying here?' An electric shock
trickled along Carradine's spine. His tone
was expressionless as he spoke.

'Why yes.' She smiled radiantly. She
looked a little surprised. 'You think that is
wrong?'

'Oh no, far from it,' Carradine said
hurriedly. 'It was just that it seemed to be
a little more than coincidence.' He eyed
her narrowly. Was there a faint look of
guilt on her face, just visible for the
briefest fraction of a second? He felt sure
he had noticed something, but it was
gone now and her gaze matched his own,

calm and challenging.

'Life is always full of coincidences, Steve. We must simply learn to live with them.' Her tone was faintly bantering.' A pause, then she went on lightly, 'But I want to help you to enjoy your stay in Montevideo. I know all of the best places to visit.' Her eyes became teasing. 'Do you like to gamble, Steve?'

'I can take it or leave it,' he said casually. Inwardly, he felt worried, but tried not to show it. The girl was keeping something from him. He felt sure of that. What it could be, he did not know, but it would not be wise to go into anything with his eyes closed.

'Good.' Valentina did not seem discouraged by his apparent lack of enthusiasm. 'I know the very place. We will have supper in a little restaurant and then go on to the club. There are so many places to see and enjoy here that it is difficult to know where to begin.'

Going back to the bed, Carradine opened one of the cases. There was a heavy Service revolver between two of the carefully-pressed shirts. It was very seldom that he ever used it; it was there more for show than anything else. With a careless man there was sometimes the chance that if he searched through the luggage and found this weapon, he did not look much further and consequently forgot completely about the other gun which Carradine carried in the shoulder holster beneath his left armpit.

Valentina moved away from the window. Almost, thought Carradine tautly, as if she had seen something — or someone — down in the street, someone she had been watching for unobtrusively.

'I'll leave you to unpack,' she said cheerfully. 'I'll call for you in an hour's time. Will that be all right?'

'That would suit me fine.' Carradine said. He waited until the girl had gone, closing the door behind her, then moved catlike to the window, pressing his body well in to the wall, glancing obliquely down into the plaza. At first, he could see nothing out of the ordinary. The girl's car was still parked outside the hotel. Then he noticed the other car, drawn up at the corner of the plaza, saw that there were two men seated in it. A little warning bell began to ring at the forefront of his mind. Although he could only just catch a glimpse of one of the men, he thought he recognized the bland features of his companion on the flight from London; the man who did not believe in statistics concerning the safety of air travel. Perhaps this too, was coincidence. As the girl had said; if so, then he would have to live with it. But a man in his profession could die because of coincidence if he was not careful. How innocent the girl had seemed — and how deadly. Brusquely, he closed his mind to her for the moment, tried to put his own thoughts into some form of order. Taking off his coat, he draped it over the back of the chair, sat down and relaxed. His mind was keyed to a razor-edged sharpness. Sooner or later, one of the FBI agents would get in contact with him. Then things ought to start moving. Always provided that he lived long enough. If the girl was a secret agent for the other side every move he made would be relayed back and plans would be made accordingly. If she was not, then it was possible he might be able to combine a little pleasure with business.

★ ★ ★

Valentina Veronova had indeed seen the black car standing at the corner of the plaza when she had looked down from Carradine's window, knew that the first part of her mission had been successfully accomplished. How much this man really suspected, she did not know for certain, but she felt sure she would soon be able to find out. Her orders had been quite explicit. Kronovitch had said they were direct from M.G.B. Headquarters in Moscow and she saw no reason to doubt that statement. Kronovitch was, she knew, high up in the organization, probably quite close to General Dernovsky. Even now, she felt an echo of that thrill of fear she had experienced when the telephone in her room at the hotel had rung that morning a little over a week earlier and she had been told to be in the Paseo del Prado, one of the public

55

gardens situated beyond the suburb of Paso Molino, some three kilometres from the city itself. It was her first meeting with Jenko Kronovitch, although she had heard of him several times. Many things had been whispered about this man, reputedly the head of the M.G.B. organization in South America. She believed most of them from the moment she heard them and after seeing him, seated in the garden, she believed the rest.

Kronovitch had looked up as she had stood a few feet from the seat, had then motioned her to sit beside him.

'Comrade Veronova.' His voice held the sharp tone of authority. 'I have recently received the reports on the work you have done for the organization since you have been in this country. Evidently, you are highly thought of in Moscow.'

Valentina had felt a sudden sense of relief flood through her, so great that for a moment she had felt certain it must have been apparent to the other, and he might have started wondering why she could have felt guilty. 'Thank you, Comrade Kronovitch.'

'There is no need to thank me. We now need you for an extremely important mission, one which must not fail. You understand that, it must not fail.'

'I understand.'

'You will have a very heavy responsibility. There is a Britsh agent coming out here with orders to destroy our organization, particularly a part of it which is working with certain military installations outside Uruguay, some five hundred kilometres from here. At the moment we do not know his identity, but that will be known to us before he arrives and you will be informed of it, so that you may meet the plane and take him into the city. He will be staying at the Hotel Uruguayo and a room has been arranged for you on the same floor as that which had been booked for him.'

'And the nature of my assignment, Comrade?' Valentina had sensed danger at that very moment, but with an effort of discipline had managed to control it, to hide it successfully.

'You will meet this man, gain his confidence, make him believe that you are a woman intent on having a good time. On the evening of the first day in Montevideo, you will take him to this address.' He passed a tiny slip of paper to her. 'We will do the rest.'

Now, eight days later, in her room at the rear of the hotel, she stood with her hands on the ledge of the window, resting her weight on her arms, trying to steady her thoughts. At the moment they refused to do what she wanted them to do. This man she had met, Steve Carradine, had not been what she had expected at all. She had been so used to the type of Russian man in the M.G.B. that she had expected him to be the same. Her mind was in a ferment and she tried desperately to remind herself that this was no time for personal things to enter into consideration. Carradine was an enemy of Russia. It was her duty to help in destroying him. She did not doubt that if he guessed at her true identity, he would do the same to her as she had been ordered to do to him, to lure him to his death. It was a time to be hard, to disclaim all romantic notions, all sentimentality.

Holding the menu in front of him, like some strange kind of weapon, the waiter led the way through the couples in the restaurant, to the table on the low balcony overlooking the main floor. The orchestra in the distance was playing one of the latest dances and every table seemed to be occupied by sun-tanned men and women, expensively dressed. Placing a smaller version of the menu he carried in his hand in front of them, the waiter snapped his fingers, bringing the wine waiter over at a rush. While Carradine ordered the wine another man hovered discreetly in the background waiting to take their order. Inwardly, Carradine felt slightly amused at everything that was happening. He had seen nothing more of those two men in the black sedan since that glimpse he had had of them early that morning. Evidently they had wanted to make sure that they knew where to find him whenever they wanted him; now they could be relying on the girl.

The meal was excellent, perfectly set off by the wine. The girl chattered gaily on every topic under the sun, the perfect companion. At times it was difficult for him to believe that she could possibly be an agent working for Russia. But his suspicions seemed too well founded for him not to believe it.

They finished their coffee. Carradine lit a cigarette, proffering the silver case to the girl, smiling a little as she shook her head slightly. 'I must confess, Valentina, that your taste in restaurants certainly appeals to me. That was one of the best meals I've ever had.'

'I'm glad you liked it.' Her smile was warm and for a moment her face bore a serious expression. Then she brightened, went on: 'But I promised you some excitement after this, did I not? Fortunately we do not have far to go. The night is warm. Shall we walk and leave my car here.'

The warning bell went again in Carradine's mind, but he nodded his head in agreement. It was clear that all this was simply the first part of the come on. Well, if that was the case, let it come. It might give him the lead he so desperately needed.

They walked slowly, side by side, along the spacious street. As the girl had said, the night was warm and the stars overhead held a soft glow. The trees were in full blossom and their scent hung heavy in the still air. Turning off the main street, they entered a narrower one, paused at the top of a small flight of stairs that led down below the level of the street. Light spilled from the windows of the room. Following the girl down the steps. Carradine thought about his suspicions concerning the girl, his feeling that she might be leading him into a trap even now. But he had seen no sign of either of the two men since they had left the restaurant itself. So if that was so, where were they?

Blinking in the harsh glare of light in the long, low-ceilinged room, he looked about him with interest. Even at that early hour, the place seemed to be unusually crowded. Card tables were spaced evenly around the room and there were several roulette wheels in operation.

'I promised you some entertainment,

some excitement, Steve,' said Valentina softly. She spread a hand expressively. 'This is it. What do you think of it?'

'Certainly it's impressive' He looked around him. Most of the upper class citizens of Montevideo seemed to be there. By day they would be on the very elite beach, or yachting beyond the harbour. At night, they came here to unwind, to lose a few thousand dollars, or perhaps gain a few hundred. It all depended on one's luck. They moved towards the nearest roulette table. The girl seated herself in one of the few vacant seats and Carradine took up his position at her shoulder. Buying chips, the girl placed them on the table in front of her.

'What is your lucky number, Steve?' she asked in a low, warm voice.

'Seven,' he said softly.

'Then tonight I shall see if it brings me luck.' Reaching out one slim hand, she placed a small stack of the coloured chips on seven, sat back.

Carradine narrowed his eyes a little. There was five thousand dollars in that tiny pile of chips. And she was letting it all ride on seven! Now where did a girl like this get that kind of money to throw around? Unless he had been mistaken about her all the time and her father was some kind of millionaire. Somehow, he did not think that could be it. She had too much reliance in her character for the usual playgirl of the upper class; was too self-confident.

The wheel slowed, the ball dropped into the seven compartment. Valentina gave a delighted cry as further chips were thrust towards her. 'You brought me luck, Steve,' she said excitedly.

'I wouldn't try it too far if I were you,' Carradine said, 'It seldom works a second time.' But it did, and a third. By this time there was a sizeable pile of chips of various colours and shapes in front of the girl. Carradine glanced down at her as she drew them in towards her, her arms enfolding them. Now, it would be the time for the big payoff. He was not quite sure why she had been allowed to win all of this money, for he felt absolutely certain that the odds against the number seven coming up three times in succession like that were so fantastically remote as not to be worth considering at all. There was something more at the back of this. Maybe it was an act on the part of the management, to pick out a beautiful woman, let her win some money like this, knowing that it would undoubtedly draw the crowds to the table — for news of a big win spread like wildfire through a place such as this — and then the odds would turn against her. She would lose everything in the next few spins.

Carradine said softly, keeping his eyes on her: 'Stop now, Valentina, while you're still ahead. Take the chips and let's get out of here.'

'But you don't understand, Steve,' she said, her eyes shining brightly in the overhead lights. 'This isn't the first time I have been here, but every other time I lost. Now that my luck has turned and I'm winning, you want me to give up and — ' She paused, bit her lip, seemed to realize that everyone, including the croupier, was waiting for her to place her bet. The wheel was ready to spin. Would the tiny ball drop into the seven compartment again?

'You're right, of course, Steve,' she said abruptly, pushing back her chair. 'But this is a lot of money. I wonder, would you be good enough to pick up the car and bring it round to the door while I change the chips?' She held out the car key for him.

'Of course.' Carradine felt the taste of the tiny victory in his mouth. He guessed that he would not be popular for this act but that did not concern him in the least. Taking the ignition key, he made his way slowly towards the door, among the card tables. He was aware of the man standing close to the door watching him through narrowed eyes. Very slowly, Carradine reached his right hand into the inside pocket of his suit, but it did not touch the top of the metal cigarette case reposing there, instead it remained close to the gun under his coat. His half-closed eyes flickered around the room for an instant, eyed the watching man again. Then he had brushed past the other, out of the door, climbing the steps up to the dark street. He had half-expected the door to open behind him while he was half-way up the steps, but it remained closed and he began to feel that there was no danger from that source. Had he been guessing wrongly all the time? Perhaps the girl was innocent of all the charges he had mentally brought against her. If that were so, he would apologize to her in due course as soon as a suitable opportunity arose. In the meantime he would enjoy her company and wait until the FBI agent contacted him. Until he met up with the other there was very little he could do. He needed all of the up-to-date information he could find. He needed to know more about this man Henkel who had supposedly been taken by the Reds. When he had that in his mind it might be possible for him to fit bits of the jigsaw together, to see if there was any recognizable picture on the canvas.

He reached the car at the side of the restaurant, opened the door and slipped in behind the wheel. Twisting the key in the starter, he listened for a moment to the soft, contented purr of the engine, depressed the clutch, closed his fingers around the gear lever and at that precise moment, a thickly-accented voice from somewhere low down on the rear seat said in his ear. 'Drive back to the club, Mister Carradine, as you were asked, but don't try to perform any heroics on the way.' The cold touch of the muzzle of the pistol against the back of his neck warned him, better than words, of the futility of doing this.

He drove the car slowly along the main street, then turned left into the narrow side-street. The houses on either side were in darkness. Shadows seemed to lie over them like a thick blanket. Out of the corner of his eye he glimpsed the yellow light that came from the room where the card games and the roulette were still in progress. He thought he saw the girl waiting on the steps as he drove up, but he couldn't be sure.

'Stop the car here,' said the harsh voice. 'No, don't try to turn round!' The muzzle of the gun dug a little deeper into the flesh of Carradine's neck. 'Get out on to the pavement and stand quite still. There is a silencer on this gun and I shall not hesitate to use it.'

Carradine knew that the other meant every word he said. He wondered which of the two men he had spotted this was. The voice did not sound like that of the man who had been seated in front of him on the plane from London.

Opening the door of the car, he stepped out, stood with his back to the car, heard the rear door open. Then the man was standing directly behind him, but Carradine knew that the other was between him and the car, that he had very little room in which to manœuvre. As if the other had suddenly realized this, he said sharply: 'Move forward, Carradine. Down the steps and then to the right, not into the club itself. We are going to have a little talk, you and I — and I do not want anyone to interrupt us.'

Obediently Carradine moved forward a couple of paces. His mind was working overtime at that moment. He knew that as soon as the girl put in an appearance any hope he may have had of getting out of this mess would be gone. His reaction was immediate and automatic. There was reason behind it. Stumbling as the muzzle of the gun was thrust into the back of his neck, just behind the left ear, he gave a small cry of pain as his leg went from under him, threw out his hands to steady himself. The man behind him gave a harsh laugh of derision, a laugh that changed quickly to a grunt of agony as Carradine swung sharply, body bent, under the arm which held the gun trained on him. In the same split second he kicked backward with his leg in a *coup de karate*. The steel-tipped toe of his shoe hit the man in the pit of the stomach. The thin, high-pitched scream that came from between his stretched lips was what Carradine had expected to hear. Before he could recover, before he could suck air down into his tortured lungs, or steady himself. Carradine swung his straightened hand, the edge hardened by long years of using this technique. There was a heavy sickening thud as it struck the other on the side of the head. The momentum of the blow rocked the other on his toes. The gun flew from his paralysed hand, clattered down the steps towards the door of the gambling club. As the man toppled backward, Carradine was on top of him, legs apart and braced on either side of his opponent's body. The man had gone down on to his knees, face contorted with agony and as he got his thumbs into the nerves on the sides of the other's neck, Carradine was able to see his face for the first time. It was one which he did not recognize. Thin, rat-like, with a long nose, eyes set a little too closely together. Now they were bulging from their sockets as he applied more pressure to the scrawny neck, lips drawn back with the air whistling in and out of oxygen-starved lungs. The man struggled ineffectually, hands upraised, clawing at the backs of Carradine's hands in an effort to loosen the strangling grip.

The tongue came out from between his teeth. He tried to make some kind of sound. Whether it was a shout for help, or a plea for mercy, Carradine did not know. He stared down dispassionately into the mottled features, increased the pressure he was exerting.

There was a soft step on the stone steps

behind him. He half turned his head, expecting it to be the girl. His gaze caught a glimpse of a man's shoe on the pavement just behind him. He heard the sudden intake of air, tried to shift his head, knowing what was undoubtedly coming.

Then the sky seemed to fall on top of him. Something hit him a crushing blow at the base of the neck and he flopped forward on to the man he had been trying to kill, rolled off the other and lay still on the pavement. A boot crashed into the side of his ribs, but he scarcely felt it.

Slowly, painfully, consciousness returned, brought in its train a stab of agony. He sucked in a deep breath automatically, and the agony spasm came again. It was strange to find himself still alive, lying on something cold and hard. A light was shining directly into his eyes and he screwed them up in a purely reflex gesture. A hand slapped him hard on the side of the face and he tried to fight against it, mouthing something which seemed to make no sense, little more than a mumble through his lips. The hand hit him again. With an effort he turned his head to the left, forced his eyes to remain open. The yellow glare in them went away, the hand stopped hitting him. Instead, he heard a voice saying urgently: 'Try to sit up, Mister Carradine. You'll feel a lot better then.'

He shook his head slowly, more in astonishment than with any other emotion. The voice held a rich American twang to it, was unlike any of the others he had heard since he had arrived in Montevideo. The quick twist of his head had hurt. For a moment the image in front of his vision blurred, receded, then came up against him so that he blinked and pulled his head back.

'Who are you?' he asked thickly. There was a rotten taste in his mouth, as if cottonwool had been thrust between his teeth, half choking him.

'I'll answer any of your questions later. At the moment I have to get you away from here. Think you can make it to my car? It's only fifty yards or so on the other side of the plaza.'

Carradine gritted his teeth, forced his

legs to obey him as the other got a hand under his armpit and pulled him to his feet. Blood pounded in his head. Going forward a couple of steps, he nearly passed out. His ribs were a mass of pain and tender, bruised flesh. There had been plenty of kicks aimed there, he thought dully. But why hadn't those men finished the job while they had been at it? Had this man come along at the wrong time for them, forcing them to leave with their task half-finished?

Somehow he made it to the car, flopped down gratefully into the seat, leaned back, his head resting on the edge of the seat, his hands loosening the collar of his shirt, sweat on his forehead and body. He did not dare to try to think at the moment. His head was one vast, throbbing ache. The other slid into the car beside him. A moment later the engine roared and the car moved forward.

3

This Drug Is Dangerous!

'You seem to have the ability to attract trouble like a fly-paper attracts flies.' The man behind the wheel turned his head slightly, grinned in the darkness, the faint flash of his teeth just showing in the shadow of his face. 'You should really be more careful in your choice of friends.'

Carradine set his teeth closely together, gave a tight smile. 'And how do you know I'm not making the same mistake again?'

The other laughed. 'With me, you mean? You couldn't be safer, my friend.' A moment later, the bantering tone vanished and he became deadly serious. 'I was ordered to contact you as soon as possible, Carradine. The name is Merton, Paul Merton. Does the name mean anything to you?'

'Merton, of course.' Carradine nodded. The FBI agent he had been detailed to

74

work with in South America! 'You must have come along in the nick of time back there. They certainly meant to finish me.'

'No doubt about that,' agreed the other. He swung the car around in a tight, side-sweeping curve, left the bright lights of the main street behind and plunged them into the semi-darkness of one of the smaller streets leading out to the suburbs. 'I think it would be best if we had a talk, just to put you in the picture. Things have been happening pretty fast down here in the past week or so, ever since they managed to snatch Henkel right from under our very noses. We had more or less got him lined up to go back to Washington with us. There was a job waiting for him at Cape Kennedy.'

'Surely any knowledge of rocketry that he may have had must have been really out of date by now. What could he possibly know that would interest you?'

'Probably very little, I guess. But the main idea behind it all was, I reckon, to make sure he was working for nobody else. So long as he was with us, we would be able to keep an eye on him.'

Was there a certain defensiveness in the other's voice? Pushing himself upright in the seat, Carradine glanced sideways. The throbbing in his head had eased a little now, had subsided into a dull ache. The other's face was just visible at intervals in the light that came from the street lamps.

'Did you see either of those men back there?'

'Only their backs,' said the other softly. He pressed down lightly on the brake, thrust the clutch deftly to the floor, bringing the car to a halt outside a tall building. At the moment it was in complete darkness.

Carradine followed Merton up the wide, stone steps, through the door which the other unlocked, along a hall, up a flight of stairs, and into the room at the end of the corridor. Merton pulled off his coat and dropped it casually over the back of a chair. He went over to the corner of the room and poured a couple of drinks. 'Scotch?' he asked.

'With ice if you have any,' Carradine replied.

'Sure thing.' There was the soft,

familiar chink of ice hitting glass, settling slowly down through the amber liquid.

Merton brought the drinks over as Carradine lowered himself on to the couch. He seated himself beside the other, one leg over the other, his left hand around his ankle in a completely relaxed pose. He seemed completely at home here.

'Now,' said Carradine, sipping the drink. 'Suppose you tell me your side of this case. I must confess, at the very beginning, that I have very little information to go on. We've been informed of what the Reds are supposed to be doing five hundred miles or so from here.'

'You can accept all of that as the truth, and a lot more besides,' nodded the other. He took a quick, almost nervous gulp of his drink. 'These people are really playing for keeps. So far, everything seems to have fallen into their laps. They've had the most fantastic luck you could possibly imagine.'

'Not luck, my friend,' Carradine corrected. 'As far as the M.G.B. is concerned, luck does not enter into their calculations. Everything is planned down to the last detail in Moscow before they even put anything into action. I happen to know a little about our friends of the M.G.B. and the N.K.V.D., which might even surprise them if they learned of it. For example, this kidnapping of Gunther Henkel, that would have been planned and arranged as much as two, maybe even ten, years ago. Their network of agents is so wide that they can call on a man to carry out even the tiniest, most trivial, act at a moment's notice anywhere in the world, just so that a kidnapping might take place without a hitch here in Montevideo.'

Merton stared at him over the rim of his glass. 'I expect you're right,' he said finally. 'Certainly as far as that part of the trouble is concerned, we've drawn almost a complete blank. Not quite the blank they wanted us to have drawn though.'

Now it was Carradine's turn to stare. 'Then you do have something to go on?'

'Henkel's daughter. Her name is Gerda. She lived with her father and a single manservant in this house in the suburbs.

It seems that even the best laid plans of mice and the M.G.B. went wrong on that occasion.'

Carradine permitted himself a slight lift of his brows. He finished the whisky, felt a warm glow begin to work its way through his stomach, expanding outward into his body. 'In what way?'

'The girl returned earlier than they had anticipated. They must have been watching the house for weeks, possibly months, making notes of everyone's movements so that they could plan the best time for the kidnapping, when Henkel was alone in the house and likely to be for some time. The last thing they wanted was to be disturbed in the act. They killed two dogs with curare. Very ingenious men these.' For a second there was a faint smile on the other's face, but it slipped instantly as he noticed the grim expression on Carradine's tight features.

'Go on,' said the other.

'Apparently, Gerda Henkel drove back to the house an hour or so before she had intended. The rehearsals of a play in which she was appearing had had to be cancelled owing to the illness of two of the cast. As she turned the corner of the road leading into the plaza, she almost ran into this car coming in the opposite direction, without any lights. Her own headlights swept over the windscreen of the other car, and she was able to make out the two men in it. One man, she felt sure, was holding a gun in his hand.'

'And the descriptions of these two men?'

'Unfortunately, we have both little to go on there, and no chance of getting anything more out of her.'

'She's dead then.' Carradine spoke quite casually, almost unconcernedly. In his profession he came face to face with death so often that it had become an everyday occurrence, something no longer treated with surprise or even reverence. The dead men and women he had seen had not looked noble as others would have liked to portray them. Death, whenever it touched anyone close to him, had always seemed such a messy thing.

'Not dead,' Merton corrected, 'although as far as helping us at all, she might just as well be dead.'

'What is that supposed to mean?' The other seemed to be talking in riddles most of the time, a thing which always tended to exasperate him.

'An attempt was made on her life the day before yesterday. Someone tried to kill her on the road. Her car must have somersaulted three or four times after it left the road. How the petrol failed to ignite is nothing short of a miracle.' He got to his feet, took Carradine's glass from him and walked back to the decanter, pouring two more drinks. Without turning his head, he went on: 'By the time the ambulance got to the scene, she had been dragged from the wreckage and laid out by the side of the road. Curiously, she suffered little more than concussion and a couple of scratches on her arm. The crash had not even marred her features.'

'Have you seen her since the accident?'

'Sure, I called in at the hospital yesterday, told the doctor in charge of the case that this was an emergency and that he could get on to the FBI Headquarters in Washington if he wanted to verify my credentials. He didn't, and he turned out to be extremely helpful, gave me all of the details of her case. Seems she may be up and about in a couple of weeks time, but that the knock she got when that car turned over, has given her amnesia. It's as complete and total a case as any he's seen. She remembers nothing prior to wakening up in hospital.'

'I see.' Carradine accepted the glass which the other thrust into his hand. He held it between his hands, looking down through the amber liquid, turning the glass gently in his hands so that the light from the bulb beneath the ceiling flashed into his eyes, reflected by the curved glass. 'Maybe if I was to see her.'

Merton looked momentarily surprised, then shook his head. 'What could you possibly do?' he asked.

'Perhaps nothing.' Carradine shrugged. 'On the other hand, I have a friend in Vienna who is an acknowledged world authority on amnesia, particularly that which is brought on by a blow on the head.' He lit a cigarette, drained his glass.

'There are certain drugs which can now be used to cure these cases.'

Merton looked dubious. 'The doctor at the hospital did not seem to have heard of them.'

Carradine smiled easily. 'Perhaps not. But I can assure you, and him, that they do exist. Naturally, there are certain dangers associated with their use, and they have not been released to doctors or hospitals. This work is purely of an experimental nature.'

'And you're suggesting that one of these drugs should be used on the girl?'

'I think that the seriousness of this trouble warrants it.' Merton was looking at him, a curious expression in his eyes. A moment later his gaze fell before the direct, penetrating stare that seemed to bore into his skull. 'Don't you?'

'I'm not sure. After all, if anything happened to her there would be a lot of terribly awkward questions that would have to be answered.'

'If we don't find a way of making her tell us everything we need to know, a lot more awkward questions are going to be asked on both sides of the Atlantic. I think we should pay a visit to this hospital as soon as possible.'

'Tonight?'

'Yes, if that can be arranged.'

Merton pursed his lips for a moment, then nodded abruptly, got to his feet and went over to the telephone in the corner. Carradine sat back on the couch and listened to the other dialling a number. A moment later he heard the other speaking quickly to someone at the other end of the wire. When he came back a few moments later, he said: 'Doctor Vandrio is on duty tonight. He will see us in fifteen minutes at the hospital. I've impressed on him the urgency of this case'

'Good.' Carradine got to his feet. 'Then I suggest that we get there right away.' Merton made a face, then nodded in agreement, finishing his drink in three gulps.

Thirteen minutes later, with Carradine glancing through the glass window that looked out along the whole length of the ward, Merton said: 'Here comes Vandrio now.'

Carradine turned, pivoting on his heels, saw the tall, thin-faced man who came into the ward, the light of the corridor behind him for a moment as he opened the door. Then he closed it softly, walked over to the small office and came in. His glance fell appraisingly on Carradine, then flickered to Merton.

'Your call sounded extremely urgent,' he said softly. 'May I ask the object of this visit at this time of night? Surely, whatever it is, it could have waited until the morning.'

Merton shrugged. 'I'm afraid this was my colleague's idea. I think he can explain.'

'Then I shall be pleased to hear the explanation, Senor Carradine. That was the name mentioned over the telephone, was it not?'

'That's right.' Carradine nodded. 'I must apologize for this urgent call, Doctor. I realize that you are an extremely busy man and I would not have asked for this meeting if there had not been other, tremendous, issues at stake.'

Vandrio wrinkled his brows a little. 'I

am afraid that I do not quite understand,' he said, looking from one man to the other. 'You ask to see me here, and also to make sure that the Night Sister is not present in this office, which is, after all, hers when she is on duty.'

'Bear with me for just a little while and I shall try to make everything clear to you, Doctor.' Carradine sat down in one of the chairs. 'No doubt you know who the girl is that we are interested in.'

'Certainly. Gerda de Silva. Her father is an extremely wealthy man.'

'Her father was kidnapped over a week ago by men we believe are Russian agents. We believe that Gerda saw them as they were driving away from the house with her father, probably unconscious, in the back seat out of sight. Because she might be able to recognize them again, or give an accurate description of them to the police, it was essential that she should not talk. I think that the man who had been ordered to kill her before she could cause any trouble, bungled the job. He should have carried it out within hours of the kidnapping. But instead, for some reason, it was several days later. He forced her car off the road, hoping that it would look like an accident and that Gerda would then be out of the way permanently. Unfortunately for them, he only succeeded in injuring her. Unfortunately for us, that injury brought on total amnesia.'

'I see.' Vandrio looked serious. 'As far as her medical history is concerned, you are correct in what you say. I know nothing about the rest. I can indeed see no earthly reason why her father should have been kidnapped by Russian agents as you would have me believe.'

'I'm afraid that this is one piece of information you will simply have to take on trust,' said Carradine stiffly. 'It would take me far too long to justify, even if I were in a position to do so.'

'Very well, I accept that.' Vandrio nodded. He spread his hands wide in a futile, resigned gesture. 'But that being the case, what do you expect me to do about it? Amnesia is one disease which cannot be cured at a moment's notice. In Gerda's case, I seriously doubt if she will ever recover her memory.' He looked up at Carradine, suddenly thoughtful. 'That was the thing uppermost in your minds, wasn't it? Whether her memory will come back so that she can tell you exactly what happened that night?'

'Not exactly. We're asking for something more than that, something more than mere information. We want her to tell us what happened this very minute.'

'That is quite out of the question. Utterly impossible,' retorted the other.

'Is it?' murmured Carradine mildly. 'On the contrary, I think that it is something which can be done, which must be done.'

Vandrio stared at him incredulously. 'May I ask how you propose to do it?'

'Have you ever heard of a drug called Valudrine, Doctor?'

'Valudrine?' Vandrio's teeth snapped shut. 'I have read a paper on this drug which was presented to the recent medical congress in Vienna, three months ago. But this is a purely experimental drug. It has never been given through clinical trials to examine any side effects which may occur with its use.'

'I agree. It is entirely possible that there may be side effects which we cannot control. On the other hand, it has been known quite conclusively, to jerk a patient out of even total amnesia in a remarkable short time.'

'I'm afraid that I must discuss this matter no further with you, Mister Carradine. It is obvious that you are not a doctor, otherwise you would never suggest using such a drug on one of my patients. I cannot allow it, of course.'

Carradine's tone was deceptively mild and soft, as he said: 'I don't think you fully recognize your position in this, doctor. Gerda de Silva's proper name is Gerda Henkel. Her father was a rocket expert, working for Hitler during the war. He came here to Uruguay less than two months after the fall of Germany, and he has been in hiding ever since. Your Government may be extremely embarrassed should this information get into the wrong hands and be published. Whether there would have been any requests for extradition. I do not know.

Certainly, the police are in trouble enough with this kidnapping. I think it would be far wiser and more discreet to do as I ask.'

Vandrio sucked in his cheeks, drawing the flesh down on to the prominent bone structure. He seemed to be debating within himself what to do for the best. Carradine said nothing. He continued to watch the other from beneath lowered lids. The man was obviously swayed by the argument he had put forward. He was not sure of the position of doctors in this country. Perhaps there was a lot of political influence behind them, and their future promotion. If that was the case, then he had a strong hold over the other and meant to use this to his greatest advantage.

Finally, Vandrio said harshly: 'This is a terrible thing that you are asking of me, Senor Carradine. If I accede to your request, then you must realize that I do so only under strong protest. It is against medical ethics to use a drug as dangerous as this, as untried as Valudrine, on a patient. She is in my care and if anything were to happen, it might be utterly impossible for me to explain it away. You realize that, of course.'

'Naturally,' said Carradine softly.

The other seemed to be considering that single word. His face was a study of mixed emotions. Then he shrugged, rubbed his hands together as if symbolically washing his hands of the whole affair.

'I will arrange for you to be taken to her ward,' he said shortly. 'And this drug which you propose to use on her. How do you intend to obtain it?'

'A plane has already been laid on to bring it from Vienna,' Carradine told him briefly. 'It will arrive here within the next twenty-four hours. Then it will be administered to her.'

Vandrio sighed. He threw a quick glance at Merton, a glowering look. 'I hope that when all of this is over you will be satisfied with what you have done,' he said tightly. 'Not that it will be of any comfort to the girl if she is dead.' He did not wait for either of them to answer, but turned quickly on his heel and walked out

91

of the office. Carradine stared at his retreating back, caught the other briefly silhouetted against the open doorway. Then the door of the ward was closed and there was only the light from two dim bulbs, one at each end of the ward, set close to the ceiling.

A small packet, doubly sealed, was waiting for Carradine at the office the next morning as Carradine, accompanied by Merton, arrived at the hospital. He opened the wrappings as he followed the nurse along the white, antiseptic-smelling corridor, to Doctor Vandrio's office on the second floor. There was a white, cardboard box, also sealed, inside the wrappings. Breaking the seals, he lifted the lid and glanced inside. The tiny ampoule of liquid rested in cotton-wool. Taking it out between his thumb and forefinger, Carradine held it up in front of him. The faintly yellow liquid inside the glass ampoule caught the light which streamed through the open windows, threw golden flashes into his eyes as he turned it slowly in his fingers.

'Is that is?' asked Vandrio.

Carradine nodded. 'Valudrine,' he said quietly. 'Now, perhaps we shall get the answers to some of our questions.'

'I hope, for your sakes, that everything goes all right,' murmured the other dubiously.

Carradine's laugh was disarming. 'The trouble with you, doctor, is that you have lived with a conservative outlook on things for so long that you refuse to accept even the need for change and advancement.'

'On the contrary,' declared the other stiffly, as he led the way out of the office, 'I'm quite prepared to accept any changes, so long as they have been tested thoroughly by clinical trials over a long enough period to detect any possible, harmful effects.'

'Sometimes circumstances can alter means.' Carradine slipped the phial back on to its bed of cotton wool, closed the lid of the box and carried it gently in his hands. They took the lift to the top floor. Inside the ward they were taken to the bed in the corner. Carradine stood at the foot of the bed and looked down at the girl who lay in it, her rich, blonde hair glistening in the sunlight. Her face was pale, high-lighted by the wide bandage, swathing around her forehead.

'Gerda,' said Vandrio softly.

The girl's eyes flicked open. She stirred under the blankets, tried to lift her head.

'Lie still,' said Vandrio. 'We are — ' He paused, then went on quickly, 'We are going to give you a small injection which will help to restore your memory. You would like that, wouldn't you?'

The girl moistened her lips with the tip of her tongue, nodded a little. Turning, Vandrio held out his hand for the box in Carradine's hands. The other handed it over to him. Taking out the phial, Vandrio broke off the top, then went around to the side of the bed where a tray of instruments had been prepared and laid out ready for use. Picking up the slender hypodermic, he thrust the needle into the phial, pulled out the plunger slowly, watching with an impassive face as the yellow liquid was sucked up into the glass barrel of the hypodermic. Squirting a little into the air, he nodded to the nurse.

Deftly she swabbed the girl's upper arm with a pad soaked in alcohol, then stood on one side as Vandrio advanced. He hesitated for a long moment, holding the hypodermic in his right hand. For a second, Carradine had the impression that he would not go through with it. Then he leaned forward over the girl, thrust the needle into the flesh of her arm and pressed home the plunger, injecting the stream of fluid into her bloodstream. Carradine waited tensely. In spite of his earlier assurances, he felt taut and apprehensive himself, although he did not intend to show it in front of the others. He watched for the girl's first reactions. At first there was nothing. The look on her face did not change. Her eyes remained expressionless.

Then he saw the slim brows draw together, the nose wrinkle across the bridge as if memory was stirring somewhere deep within her mind, breaking through the barrier which had been imposed by her subconscious, blocking off all memory of the incidents prior to the crash. He saw her lips move, saw her struggle once more to rise in the bed, her eyes widening a little.

'Gerda,' said Carradine softly. 'Do you remember who you are?'

'Gerda Henkel,' she said in a soft voice. For a moment it was as if she were merely reciting lines which she had learned parrot-fashion. Then a new quality came into her tone, a crowding fear which threatened to blot out everything else. Her voice was lifted in volume and pitch as she went on: 'My father! What have they done with my father?'

'Don't worry about that, Gerda, for the moment,' said Carradine, his voice reassuring. 'We need you to help us get him back. Those two men you saw. Can you describe them to us, as closely as you can.'

'I saw them in the light of the headlights,' she said tonelessly. 'One man had a gun. They must have had my father in the rear seat, either tied up or unconscious. If only I had known then what had happened, I might have been able to follow them, to have done something. But even after I got back to

96

the house, even after I discovered he was not there, I thought nothing about it until I found the two dogs. They had been killed by some kind of poison.'

'The two men,' said Carradine insistently. 'What of them?'

'One man was huge. He was driving the car. His face was like that of an animal, almost. The other, the man with the gun was thinner, his face pinched, a long nose, eyes set close together.'

'Could you recognize them if you saw either of them again. Or a photograph of them?'

'Yes, I think so.'

'Good. This has been a great help to us. If there is anything else you may think is important — '

The girl was silent for a long moment, her eyes staring up at the ceiling, her lips twisted. She looked terrified of something. 'The other car,' she said in a halting tone. 'The man who tried to kill me, who forced me off the road.'

'Yes,' said Carradine quietly.

'He was the man I saw in that first car, the man with the gun.'

97

* * *

Steve Carradine woke early the next morning in his room at the Hotel Uruguayo, absently, he reached out and checked the gun under his pillow, then rolled over and swung his legs to the floor. Going over to the window, he glanced down into the street, half expecting to see the black limousine there again at the corner of the plaza, but it was not in sight. Had they decided to call off their watchdogs after last night? If so, then their actions were, to say the least of it, premature. Somehow, he did not think that men as methodical as those of the M.G.B. would be content with simply believing they might have killed him in that attack outside the gambling club. It was more likely they would send someone to make certain.

He was not disappointed. Less than five minutes after he had dressed and shaved, there was a soft knock on the door of his room. It opened before he called out.

'I was hoping that you were awake.'

Valentina Veronova came into the room, closing the door behind her. She pouted at him as she seated herself on the edge of the sofa, one nylon-sheathed leg swinging idly. 'I have, as you say in England, a bone to pick with you.'

Carradine lifted his brows a little, said nothing, waiting for her to go on. He had scarcely expected to see the girl again after what had happened the previous night, but he was quite prepared to play along with this, just so long as he was doing it with his eyes open, forewarned.

'When you left me at the Club, I expected you to come back with the car to pick me up. But you never returned. I waited for perhaps fifteen minutes and then went out to look for you. The car was there all right, but there was no sign of you What happened?'

'Don't you know?' Carradine said tightly.

'But of course I don't know How could I? I was in the Club waiting for you to pick me up, clutching the best part of a small fortune in my hands. I suppose anyone could have come along.'

'Now listen to me, Valentina,' Carradine's tone was low and deadly. 'Quite a lot happened last night after I left you to pick up the car. A good deal of it seemed too much of a coincidence to be anything less than a well-prepared plan to have me put out of the way permanently.'

Her eyes widened at his words. For a moment her lips were parted in obvious surprise. Was it just a little too obvious? Or did she really not understand?

She said indifferently. 'I wish I knew what you are talking about, Steve. If this is an excuse for your actions last night, then I'd like to hear it.' Turning, she lowered herself gracefully on to the couch, one leg crossed over the other. There was no expression on her face now.

'Very well. I'll explain. I got your car from the parking lot outside the restaurant, but there was a visitor there already, a Russian agent with a gun. He forced me to drive here, then to get out. He said that he would be waiting for someone and implied that when this person arrived, I would be taken for a drive, out into the country where I could be murdered without any witnesses. Unfortunately for him, and his companion, I also had an accomplice waiting, although I didn't know it at the time.'

She regarded him steadily, unblinkingly, for several moments. Then she said tautly, through her teeth. 'You're not saying that I had anything to do with what happened to you, are you? I was in the Club all of that time. I knew nothing about any attempt that was to be made on your life. Or is it just that because I am Russian you — '

'Caucasian,' said Carradine softly, a grin on his lips. There were tears showing in the girl's eyes, but no trace of guilt on her face. Had he misjudged her? It certainly looked that way.

'Is that what you think? That I'm one of *them*.' Deliberately, she stressed the last word, made it sound like an unclean taste in her mouth.

'I'm sorry, Valentina. At the moment, I don't know what to think. But somehow, they knew that it was your car, and they were waiting for me to go back for it. Too many events seemed to have combined to make it seem just a coincidence.'

Valentina seemed to make up her mind. Nodding her head quickly, she wiped her eyes with the back of her hand. There was no ultra-feminine dabbing of her eyes with a wispy handkerchief, Carradine noticed. Then she looked straight at him her jaw thrust forward a little. 'You've got to believe me,' she said with a forced quietness 'I had nothing to do with these people. Nothing at all.'

Carradine nodded easily. 'Then we will forget it,' he said, his voice calm and casual. 'Now, have you had breakfast yet?'

'No, I was hoping that you would join me.'

'I'd be delighted.'

Breakfast was excellent. Carradine, having been in this country once before knew beforehand what to expect, and by the time the hot coffee arrived, was feeling pleasantly full. Relaxing his body, he glanced up, saw Merton standing just inside the doorway of the dining room. The other's gaze fell on him and he walked over, paused at Carradine's side, looking across the table at the girl. 'I can see that you have already availed yourself of one of the delights of this city, Carradine,' he said, bowing slightly in Valentina's direction.

'This is Valentina Veronova,' Carradine said, introducing the girl. 'Paul Merton.'

'How do you do, Senor Merton.' The girl watched the American's thoughtful face.

Merton bowed again from the waist, then flickered his gaze at Carradine. 'I hate to drag you away from so charming and beautiful companion,' he said urgently, 'but I'm afraid I must. This business is of extreme importance. I'm sure that Miss Veronova will excuse you.'

'Of course.' The girl seemed to turn something over in her mind, then pushed back her chair and rose to her feet. 'I must change my dress if I am to go into the city to do some shopping.'

Merton waited until she had gone, then slipped into the chair she had just vacated, looked about him to ensure that they could not be overheard, lowered his voice as he said softly: 'That girl. She was the one you were with last night?'

'Yes. I told her most of what happened when I went to collect her car. She denied having any part in it, of course.'

'But you said nothing about our visit to the hospital, or about the drug and what we learned from Gerda Henkel.'

'Of course not. There's always the chance that she is one of them.'

'A very good chance, I would say,' murmured the other. 'But to get to the point of my visit here, I've checked through most of the files we have on known Russian agents in this part of the world, took a few with me to the hospital. Gerda picked out one of them right away as the man who had been driving that car.'

'Go on,' said Carradine flatly. His voice was casual.

'His name is Jenko Kronovitch, one of the top men in the M.G.B. He hasn't been in Uruguay long. I think he must have been sent here direct from Moscow a short while ago, possibly to superintend operations here.'

'But you've got no lead on the other man?'

'None at all. We're still checking through the files. If that doesn't produce results quickly, I'll try to get the girl out of that hospital and into our Headquarters here where she can have a go with the Identigraph.'

'That ought to help.' Carradine nodded. It had been used successfully on several occasions in London, and was now standard equipment at Secret Service Headquarters as well as at New Scotland Yard. Basically, it was a device for recording the major items of a person's features, skull, hair, nose, eyes and mouth, each item being taken from a stock of items and superimposed on the basic characteristics already chosen. In the end, a sort of composite picture was built up which was almost invariably found to give a reasonable likeness to the person in question. From a fleeting glimpse, seen in a dark street, a good likeness could often be built up.

'I've got men looking for Kronovitch right now. If he's around here anywhere I reckon it won't be long before they get a lead on him.'

'But we're no further forward with finding out where they've taken Henkel.'

'Afraid not. We've got to work this out. At the moment our chances are not good. They've got this site so well hidden that so far, we haven't even been able to get a smell at it.'

'Yet you're pretty sure that it's somewhere to the west of here, possibly not in Uruguay.'

'Almost certainly, it's not in Uruguay. I doubt if the Uruguayan Government would allow it. They're too friendly with the United States. This would finish them completely and they know it. I think we can take it that they are as anti-Communist as we are.'

'Then there's only one way to do this as I see it. One of us must get into that site, find out everything possible. It's only there, I'm sure, that we can get any information on how they propose to bring those nuclear warheads into the country.'

'Well, I think that's crazy,' said the other, shaking his head dubiously. 'It won't be easy getting inside. They must have it so well guarded that an army would be needed to break in.'

'Not if we got in as workmen. They must have men working on the site. That way, we should be able to discover something.'

Merton smiled mirthlessly. 'They are not fools, you know, Carradine. We've been on to them for some time now and believe me, they're as cunning as they come. I think we can take it that every man who works there will have been thoroughly screened before he gets within a hundred miles of the place. Even then, he'll be watched every second of the day, probably locked inside some sleeping quarters at night, paraded to work in the morning, and returned to what is virtually a prison when the work is finished.'

'That's a risk which will have to be taken. Besides, it's certain that they have taken Henkel there. He'll probably be used to help them in the assembly of the rocket warheads. When his usefulness is finished, they'll kill him to make certain that he doesn't talk.'

'All right.' The other was still obviously unconvinced. He added harshly: 'They warned me before I met you that you were a man who always met trouble more than halfway. Now I know they were right. I suppose you've reckoned on the danger there is, the fact that if Henkel is there, so is our friend Kronovitch and he knows you by sight.'

Carradine looked composed. He said softly: 'You have no faith, Paul. In this business it is essential to have faith, otherwise you would get nowhere.'

'Is there anything I can do to help?'

Carradine looked casually up. He said: 'You seem to have a good organization here in Montevideo. Can you get your men to find out whether anyone here is hiring labour for work outside the city. Whoever it is, it will be someone looking for a large force of men. I doubt if you'll mistake the agency once you locate it.'

Merton scraped back his chair. He nodded. 'I'll get somebody on to that right away. I figure it ought to be possible to have some kind of an answer by tonight at the latest. Maybe you'd better come to my place. They may have this hotel watched.' He paused, then said thinly: 'I'd also check that room of yours if you haven't already done so. They may not be content simply to rely on the girl.'

Carradine tightened his lips, nodded. 'I'll do that,' he promised. 'Thanks for reminding me. In the meantime, do your best to get that information.' He fingered the white card which the other handed to him, glanced down at the neatly printed address. 'And I'll contact you tonight, say at nine o'clock. That should give you twelve hours to find this agency.'

'Will do,' said the other calmly.

Going back to his room, Carradine found that the bed had been made, the ashtrays cleared, in his absence. Everything about this hotel seemed remarkably efficient, carried out unobtrusively. One scarcely ever saw the servants who cleaned the rooms. He recollected that he had seen a chambermaid once in his travels along the maze of corridors in the hotel, during the short period he had spent discovering the lay-out of the place. It was something he always did when first going into a new hotel. It was so easy to lose one's way, wander for fifteen minutes or so along the corridors before getting back to one's room. He had already discovered that Valentina Veronova had booked into the hotel the day before he had arrived.

Inside the room, he looked about him with a more than casual interest, is keen gaze taking in everything, eyeing it with a second look. The flowers on the table close to the bed. A swift check assured him there was no small button microphone hidden there, no thin, almost invisible wires leading down from the vase, along the leg of the table and into one of the room on either side of him. The bed was innocent of anything suspicious. So, too, were the table and the chairs placed with a meticulous care around the room. He went into the adjoining bathroom, found nothing out of place. The small cupboard on the wall above the bath with the glass doors revealed nothing. Shrugging his shoulders, he went back into the room. There seemed to be absolutely nothing. Yet as Merton had reminded him, these people usually left nothing to chance, always tried to back up one of their methods of keeping tabs on someone, with another. He sharpened his senses abruptly, tried to recall all of the methods he had known to be used in the past.

There was something wrong here, he felt certain of that. But what could it be? Some object out of its normal place, even by an inch or so? Something, however innocent, which ought not to be where it was? There seemed to be literally a hundred possibilities. Out of the corner of his eye he caught the bright glare of sunlight reflected from the mirror on the wall across from the bed. Yes, that was it!

Slowly, he walked over to it, ran his finger over the smooth glass surface. Even from close to, it looked quite ordinary but there was a curious dull sheen to it when viewed from a slightly acute angle. He had seen that bloom behind the glass of a mirror on one or two occasions in the past, knew that it was a one-way mirror, that although he could see nothing through it from that side, a man standing on the other side of the glass would be able to look into the room and see all that was happening. Now if he was right in this surmise —

Placing his fingers around the bevelled edge, he tried to ease it away from the wall. It was fixed solidly into the plasterwork. Lifting his fingers a little higher he felt around the edge, felt that tiny object near the top edge of the mirror. At first sight, even on a reasonable, close inspection, it would appear to be nothing more than part of the rich ornamentation around the edge of the mirror, but his sensitive fingertip could just feel the small length of wire that led back from it into the wall. It was remarkably well made, even for an object of this type. A cunning blend of the one-way mirror and a small button microphone, feeding both vision and sound into the room next to his. He did not need anything else to tell him that one of the Russian agents of the M.G.B. occupied that room, no matter what name would be signed in the register downstairs. His jaws clenched tightly. Taking the long-bladed knife from along his wrist, he took one of the chairs over to the wall just beside the mirror, stood on it carefully, and inserted the strong blade of the knife just below the button microphone, where it was joined on to the rest of the mirror. A quick twist of his wrist and the wires leading back into the wall had been cut through. Grinning a little to himself, he got down from the chair. Now all he had to do was drape his jacket over the mirror whenever he wished and he had effectively destroyed their eyes and ears.

He was beginning to realize how tricky and resourceful these men were. He doubted if they had learned much so far by means of this device, but if he had not discovered it, there was no telling what they might have learned and with the girl skilfully pumping him, it could have been the end of the plan he had laid.

Going over to the drink tray which had been thoughtfully provided, he mixed a Scotch and soda, went across to the chair near the window and lowered himself into it, staring down into the busy street below him as he lit a cigarette and drank the whisky slowly. Everything that had been done by these men so far had been performed with skill. They were not amateurs. They had learned their lessons in sabotage well in Russia, one of the toughest schools in the world. A man who failed, no matter how trivial that failure might be, was doomed. He would be taken back to Russia and his fate would have already been decided before he left the country.

He blew smoke out in front of him, watched the traffic narrowly down below. As far as he was concerned, he had better make sure that no further mistakes were made. He had almost lost his life earlier and it had been only the timely intervention of Paul Merton which had saved him. There would have to be nothing more like that in the future, if there was to be a future for him.

4

Death of an Agent

Carradine's footsteps echoed back at him from the tall buildings on either side of the narrow street. The warm night of the Southern Hemisphere hung over the city, a deep purple, already lit by thousands of stars, unfamiliar and strange constellations that winked at him in a pattern of light. There seemed to be no one about, even at this early hour of the night, unless they had all decided to stick to the main thoroughfares of the city. Here, he was in the old sector, built on that promontory which thrust itself out into the sea. From the first, this part of Montevideo had given him the impression of being a place where it was not wise to walk alone after dark. In contrast to the newer part of the city, there were many dark streets here where death could come swiftly out of the shadows. It reminded him, in places, of some of the cities of the Orient. There was that same, indefinable air of mystery, of brooding fear, lying over the low houses, lurking in the pools of shadow which seemed to smother most of the street on both sides.

His instinct told him that this part of Montevideo was one in which it was possible that he might not get out alive. Why in hell had Merton chosen to give him an address here? Was it that after what had happened, the other wanted to be super-cautious? Was he taking no chances on Carradine being followed? Perhaps he was seated at some window at that very moment, where he could look along the whole length of the street, could see him walking along the narrow pavement, could see clearly whether there were any other dark shadows lurking at his heels. He paused momentarily, listened intently for the quiet pad of feet at his back. But there was no sound. It was as if the whole place was asleep, but fitfully asleep, with one malevolent eye still open, watchful for trouble.

Keeping well away from the wall, he

116

walked on down the long, narrow boulevard, eyes flicking from one side to the other, his body poised so that he could twirl and twist in any direction in a split second if danger threatened. It was the walk of a man who had lived with danger, who knew how to meet it if it came. He thought of the time he had had in London before he had been given this assignment and wished that he was back there, and wondered what trouble he was going to run into on this mission. There seemed to be far too many intangibles and improbables around for his liking.

For five minutes he walked on in silence with only the echo of his own footsteps to keep him company. The moon sailed out from behind a low stretch of cloud, turned it into a sheet of mother-of-pearl for a moment as it broke free, then flooded the street ahead of Carradine with a white light. If anything, it made things worse, deepened the shadows on either side and formed new ones. Lifting the piece of card to his chest, Carradine glanced down at it once more, checking on the address printed there, although he knew it by heart now. The next turning but one on the left, halfway along the street. A car turned the corner of the long boulevard behind him. The headlights shone along the street and he moved deeper into the shadows as the beams came searching along the boulevard. He pressed himself into a niche between two of the buildings. The car drew level with him. Without any change in the note of the engine, it went on past. He caught a brief glimpse of the man seated behind the wheel, a cigar between his lips. He did not recognize him. Certainly it was none of the M.G.B. agents he had met so far. Waiting until the car had gone out of sight around the corner half a mile further on, he stepped out into the street, moved a little more quickly now, turned into the second opening on his left. The alley was little more than ten feet wide, with the dark buildings lifting high on either side. Not a sound broke the stillness. The buildings successfully shut out the moonlight here and there was the stench of garbage in his nostrils as he went forward carefully, placing one foot in front of the other, setting them down gently. Turning his head slightly, he focused his eyes on the buildings on his right. Was that a faint glow of light, showing through thin, flimsy curtains at one of the windows? He paused, stood absolutely still to make sure. There was no doubt about it now, a greyish, blurred glow that stood out against the blackness of the houses now that he knew where to look. This was the place. A quick glance behind him. There was no one there, and he felt sure that nobody had turned into the alley from the boulevard.

Swiftly, he moved across to the house, knocked softly on the door. The stillness persisted. Cautiously, he lifted his hand and knocked again. The echoes moved through the house, but evoked no response. Putting up his palm to the door, he pushed gently. It swung open on creaking hinges. A tingle went along his spine as he stood there. There was something wrong here. At the moment he was not sure what it was. This was certainly the house. The number was on the wall just beside the half open door.

Slipping inside, he eased the gun from the shoulder holster, pushed off the safety catch. His eyes were now accustomed to the darkness. A dingy hall opened out in front of him and he padded noiselessly along it. He guessed that the light he had seen came from a room leading off the right of the hall and a moment later, he spotted the door leading into the room. Gently, he turned the knob, pushed. The door swung open. A lamp was burning on the table in the middle of the small room. It threw shadows into the corners, touched the cracked mirror on the wall, the threadbare carpet on the floor, and the shoes and legs of the man who lay sprawled there, the rest of his body in the shadow thrown by the low table.

Holstering the gun, Carradine moved forward, went down on one knee beside the man on the floor and gently turned him over. It was Paul Merton. The American agent was still alive, but only just. There was a trickle of blood on his lips and his head was thrust back, there was a spreading red stain on the front of his shirt, around the hilt of the knife which had been thrust into his body just below the breastbone.

As Carradine moved him the eyes flickered open for a brief moment, the lips twitched into a travesty of a smile.

'Who did it?' said Carradine thinly. 'Can you tell me who it was?'

He saw the muscles of the other's throat cord and writhe as he tried to speak. His lips moved and more blood trickled down his face and chin. The tongue touched the back of the parted teeth, then he said in a hoarse, hurried whisper, the words all slurring together as he tried to get them out, to shape them into sensible sounds: 'Small man, thin-faced. Must have been . . . ' He swallowed convulsively, drew in a deep shuddering breath that brought a further spasm of agony to his features, 'must have been the other . . . man. The man Gerda saw with the gun.'

Carradine listened with tightening lips. There was nothing he could do now for this man. Obviously he was so close to death that the slightest touch could stop his heart for ever. Yet there were so many things he felt this man knew which it was essential for him to know if he was to succeed in this mission.

'That agency? Did you find anything?'

Merton tried to nod his head, but could only move it a few inches. His body relaxed and for a moment Carradine felt sure the other was dead. Then Merton opened his eyes again. There was a glaze forming on them. 'In the top drawer, there . . . ' The other lifted his hand, managed to point to the far side of the room.

Lifting his eyes, Carradine saw the chipped set of drawers, nodded to the other to indicate that he had understood what he was trying to say.

A moment later the other uttered a low sigh that came out from between his tightly clenched teeth. His back arched for a second into an impossible posture, then he was still. The lines of pain were smoothed from his face and the eyes remained open, staring sightlessly up at the cracked and peeling ceiling. Automatically, Carradine felt for the pulse.

There was no beat under his finger and he slowly placed the arm on top of Merton's body.

Pushing himself up to his knees, he squatted there for a moment staring down into the face of this man who had saved his life once, but whom he had not been able to save. He ought to have guessed that sooner or later, the Red organization would get to Merton. Whether they had connected the American with him, or with the Henkel affair mattered little. All that was important was that they had known who he was, and they had taken the necessary steps to see that he no longer represented any danger to them.

Getting to his feet, he walked brusquely over to the chest of drawers, opened the top one. There were a couple of carefully-folded shirts there and a dark tie resting on top of them. He searched through the shirts found nothing. The rest of the drawer seemed to be empty, yet the other had said that the information was here. He examined the articles of clothing once again, more closely this time, found what he was looking for a few moments later. It had been slipped carefully into the fold of the tie. Opening out the single piece of paper, he went back to the table and held it close to the dim lamp, scanning the lines of writing. The address given was in one of the suburbs of Montevideo. *The Aroyo Mining Corporation*. That seemed as good a front as any for an organization such as this, he thought grimly. Tomorrow, in his guise of a Uruguayan workman, he would try to get them to give him a job, anywhere so long as it was outside of the city. If he suggested a somewhat shady past, it might be an advantage to him. These people preferred those working for them to have something in their background which they could use as blackmail if the necessity for such a manoeuvre ever arose.

He turned, thrust the paper into his pocket, glanced down at the dead body of Paul Merton lying on the floor. What to do about him? he wondered. Ring the police and tell them there was a dead man at this address, a man who had been murdered. It seemed the only logical solution. Perhaps it might be the best thing to do. Certainly the other members of the American organization in the city would then be warned of what had happened and might be able to take steps to protect themselves.

Carefully, he let himself out of the room. The hallway was silent, dark, the paper faded and peeling from the walls in places. The automatic made a reassuring bulge against his side. Going out into the alley, he glanced up and down the street, searching the shadows for any sign of movement. A cat raced from one shadow to another, came rushing towards him, saw him and swerved off to one side, uttering a low mewing wail as it vanished into the night. He forced his quivering nerves to calm.

There was the feel of danger here. His nerves jumped a little as he edged forward, away from the house, moving towards the entrance of the alley some fifty yards away. He could just make out the dim line of moonlight which fell obliquely across the alley mouth, although none of it managed to penetrate any further. It was as if even the moonlight shunned this place of evil.

Twenty yards from the end of the alley, the sudden sharp scrape of a boot on the cobbled stones caught his ear. He whirled towards the sound, instinctively and catlike, made no attempt to reach for his gun. He did not want to bring anyone else here by the sound of gunfire. Besides, it might be the man who had killed Merton, a man who had stayed there in case anyone else did show up. The shape launched itself out of the shadows of one of the buildings, hurtling across the six feet of space towards Carradine. He saw the arm upraised to throw, caught the faint glint of light on the naked blade. The knife sighed past his head as he ducked swiftly. He heard it strike the wall behind him and clatter to the road. Then the man was on him in a sudden rush, one arm snaking out for his throat, seeking to take a strangling grip on him. Carradine let the other come on, knowing that his momentum could be used against him. He turned, caught at the other's outthrust arm, pivoted sharply, pulled on the other's body. The man went flying over his bent shoulder and hit the ground hard. Even as he fell, Carradine had moved. A couple of strides brought him behind the man, as the other was struggling fiercely to rise, shaken by the impact of his fall. Going down on to one knee, Carradine hooked one arm around the man's throat and began to squeeze slowly, exerting pressure on the other's windpipe, cutting off the other's breath. The man began to struggle, quite ineffectually against the choking arm across his throat. His eyes began to bulge in their sockets, his tongue thrusting out between the parted lips.

'Who are you?' Carradine hissed. 'Are you going to tell me?'

The other said nothing, continued to struggle. Gently, Carradine lifted his other hand, found the nerve in the side of the man's neck, just below the right ear. He pressed slightly on it, not enough to kill the man, although that would have been the result had he increased the pressure just a little more, and knew that the other was experiencing excruciating agony, a splitting pain in his skull.

'Are you going to speak now?'

A pause, then the other nodded his head as far as he could with Carradine's arm around it, the elbow on the adam's apple. He relaxed the pressure on the other's throat slightly. 'All right. But no tricks or I'll kill you, you understand?'

Another nod. 'Very well. What are you doing here and why did you try to kill me?'

'I thought you were somebody else,' was the croaking reply. 'A friend of mine was attacked last night in this alley. I waited here for his attackers. When I saw you coming, I thought you were one of them.'

Carradine brushed the rest of the other's words aside contemptuously. 'Why do you persist in lying?' he said thinly. He jerked his arm back into a tight hold again. 'You were in that house across the alley earlier. You killed the man who lived there with a knife. I notice you're good at throwing knives. It must have been that. You would never have taken him by surprise and killed him in fair fight. Then you waited until you saw me go in, knew that I was sure to find his body, and that you would have to kill me too, to prevent me from talking.'

Threshing wildly with his arms, the man tried to break free. A horrible gurgling came from deep within his tortured throat. The wind whistled sharply in and out of his mouth. Reaching up, he tried to claw Carradine's arm away from his throat, nails raking deep bloody furrows in the flesh. But Carradine held on grimly. He doubted if the other would tell the truth even if threatened with death. The members of the M.G.B. back in Moscow had tortures far worse than any that he could dream up for this man, and once word got through to them that he had talked, these men, the executioners of the organisation, would see to it that he suffered the tortures of the damned-on-earth before he died, screaming and pleading for death to come and release him from his agonies.

He thought momentarily of Merton, lying there in that room, thought of the manner in which he had died, and there was no compassion whatever in his mind as he jerked back on the other's neck. The man uttered a little cry, a faint bleat of agony. Then his body collapsed limply in Carradine's grasp. Releasing his hold on the other, he got to his feet as the man dropped on to his face in the dirt. He lay quite still, unmoving, his neck broken. Glancing about him, Carradine saw that there was no movement in the whole length of the alley. Evidently there had been only the one of them. He had obviously been sent out to carry out this job with orders to wait in case anyone else showed up and tried to contact Merton. If that happened, then this person, too, was to be eliminated.

For a second, he stared down at the shape on the ground, then turned and walked quickly and noiselessly out of the long alley, into the boulevard. By daylight, there would be no trace of that man back there. When he failed to make an appearance at their headquarters in the city, wherever that might be, someone would be sent out to check on him and his body would be quickly and quietly removed, snatched from sight before the police, or anyone else started asking awkward questions around town.

Slowly, he made his way through the moonlit, deserted streets. More than ever before, the feeling of evil and danger, grew in his mind. By the time he reached the Hotel Uruguayo, he felt oddly worried. Things were beginning to get out of control. If he had been able to force that man to talk, he might know a little more of what was going on inside the Red organisation. He might even have been able to get a few details of what their plans were for him. By now, they must be getting pretty desperate about him. They had failed once, twice counting tonight, and they could not be sure how much he had learned from Merton, before they had finally succeeded in silencing the other.

It was just possible, though, he reflected, as he stripped and stood under the cold shower in the bathroom, that he could turn this to his own advantage. Desperate men were inclined to do rash things, to make mistakes which cool-headed men never did. It only needed them to make one mistake and he might have them just where he wanted them. In the meantime, he would have to lay his plans with care, and get himself accepted as a workman at this secret building site where the launching base was being prepared.

Back in the bedroom, he checked that the coat which he had thrown over the mirror was still in position, that not a single glimpse of what went on in the room would be visible to the men, waiting and watching on the other side. How long before they realised that it was not something wrong with the mechanism of the mirror, but that he had tumbled to their trick, he did not know. Even when they did find out, there would be very little they could do about it. It was unlikely that they would enter the bedroom when he was out and mend the instrument. On the other hand, they might place some other concealed microphone here, hoping that he would be too flushed with the victory of having discovered the mirror that he would fail to look any further and in particular that he would not check things twice.

The telephone on the bedside table rang softly. He stared at it for a moment, then went over and picked it up. 'Room one-three-six,' he said quietly.

'Steve.' Valentina's voice. 'I was looking for you earlier this evening. I thought you might have liked to have gone out to dinner with me. But you were nowhere about. I think it mean that you didn't tell me you were going out.'

'I'm sorry, Valentina. But something important came up and I couldn't postpone it.'

'Then why don't I come across and have a drink now?' There was the slightest trace of coquetry in her voice. 'There's more than an hour left yet and I feel I must have someone to talk to for a little while.'

'All right. I'll have a drink mixed by the time you get here.'

There was a soft click as the receiver on the other end of the line was replaced in its cradle. He put his own phone down, sat for a moment turning things over in his mind. Now why had she suggested a talk at this time of night? And had she really wanted to go out to dinner when she had come looking for him, or had she been trying to keep watch on him. It must have irked when she had been unable to find him anywhere and she had realised that he had slipped through her fingers. How could that be explained to her superiors? He tied his tie in a loose knot, surveyed himself in the mirror of the dressing table. He tried to put these dark suspicious thoughts concerning the girl out of his mind. He had been almost convinced that morning at breakfast that she had had no part in these intrigues. But now, all of his earlier suspicions about her came back to him with a rush. There were so many little, unexplainable things which just did not seem to fit in with the general picture she wished to convey to him, little things which jarred whenever he tried to think of them objectively. He went over to the window and pulled the curtain a little on one side, feeling the cool night air swirl briefly around him. He looked at the watch on his wrist. It was nearly eleven o'clock.

The soft knock on the door sounded just as he had finished mixing a cocktail and he went over and opened the door. Valentina came in, smiling up at him. She wore a yellow dress, with a wide black belt around her slender waist. Her hair was in a loose knot and her eyes surveyed him gravely as he stood on one side to let her in. Closing the door behind her, he watched her every movement as she walked into the room. He saw the quick look that she threw in the direction of the mirror on the wall. Then she had turned and there was a look of puzzled bewilderment on her delicate features.

'Why have you done that, Steve?'

'Done what?' he inquired innocently. He looked down at the cocktail shaker in his hand. 'I thought you wanted a drink and someone to talk to.'

'I mean the mirror. You've put a coat over it. Surely you can't be as averse to your own reflection as that.'

'Not exactly. But it's one of my

idiosyncracies. I don't like too many mirrors in a room. The one on the dressing table is enough for me.'

She shrugged nonchalantly, seemed to dismiss the matter from her mind as she walked over to the couch, sat down, looked up at him, then patted the seat beside her. 'Come and talk to me, Steve,' she said softly, provocatively. 'I've been lonely all day with no one to talk to.'

'I'll mix the drinks first,' he said, smiling. 'Business before pleasure. Or don't you have that motto in Russia.'

'Of course.' Her smile was devoid of any emotion. She lit a cigarette and leaned back, one arm resting across the back of the couch. 'What did you do tonight that was more important than having dinner with me?'

Although her tone was light and bantering, he thought he detected a note of serious inquiry in it. 'I thought that you were here mainly on pleasure.'

'I only wish that were true. Unfortunately, I'm here mostly on business. My firm sent me out here to keep a general eye on their affairs. That means that I shall make my headquarters here in Montevideo, but that I may often have to leave and go out into the country.'

She pouted, her lower lip pushing forward a little. 'Just when I thought that you and I were going to get on very well, you tell me that you may be leaving soon. Not too soon, though, I hope.'

'Very soon, I'm afraid.' Carradine brought the glasses over to the couch, handed one to her, then sat down on the cushions beside her. The faint perfume of her hair came to him as she leaned a little closer to him. Her face was incredibly beautiful. Carradine examined it coolly and she lowered her glance a moment later, a faint red flush suffusing her cheeks.

'When do you have to go?' she asked softly.

'Perhaps tomorrow,' he said, sipping the drink. 'It depends on whether I can get in touch with my associates in the country. It could be that they cannot find time to talk to me right away. In which case, I shall be only too pleased to have dinner with you every possible night.'

She smiled at that, looked at him over the rim of her glass. Her expression was serious. 'I should like that, Steve.' She raised her glass. 'Here's to a very long and flourishing friendship between us.'

5

The Night Holds Danger

It was the afternoon of the next day.

During the morning, Carradine had checked out as much as was known of the Aroyo Mining Corporation. On the face of things, it appeared to be a legitimate concern, operating various small, but apparently rich, mines in the outer reaches of Uruguay. The office was situated in one of the industrial estates on the outskirts of Montevideo, had been registered is the normal way, and would, he felt sure, bear the closest scrutiny from any of the Government Departments. If Merton had been correct with his information, these people had been devilishly clever and thorough in their work. Nothing here to connect in any way with what was going on five hundred miles to the west.

After taking a bath and shower,

Carradine changed his clothes. He toyed with the idea of taking his gun or not, finally deciding to leave it. He had no intention of fighting his way into the secret building sites. There was only one way to get in which offered any chance of success, as one of the native workmen, hired by the Aroyo Mining Corporation. Certainly his command of the language, inherited from his Spanish mother, would be sufficient for him to pass muster.

Ten minutes later, he rang the desk of the hotel, informed the receptionist that he would be leaving Montevideo on business for possibly a week or a fortnight, but that he wished his room to be kept for him, that he was leaving most of his luggage behind. Once these arrangements had been made, he left the floor by the fire escape and was down in the street at the rear of the Hotel Uruguayo within two minutes, unseen by anyone in the hotel, unrecognisable now from the hundreds of other men in the street, the clothes he wore perhaps a little shabbier than most, the wide-brimmed straw hat pulled well forward, shading the tanned, aquiline features. The long-bladed knife was still strapped to his wrist, the shoes he wore, a little heavier and thicker than normal, each housing a razor-sharp blade, but this difference would only be noticed on extremely close examination, by someone who knew what he was looking for.

He followed his route of that morning, when he had made his way to the suburb of Montevideo to examine the registered offices of the Aroyo Mining Corporation from a distance. Now it was time for the last lap. Outwardly, he was just another of the hundreds of out-of-work men in the city. The face which looked back at him from the glass of a nearby window was nondescript, so well made up that he had little fear of being recognised, if he should be so unfortunate as to bump into any of the men who had tried to kill him.

The Mining Corporation's offices, a heavy, ugly sort of building, stood between two taller buildings, both apparently empty and deserted. Possibly by design, Carradine reflected grimly, their owners bought out so that there might be no one close by to keep a watch on any of the activities of the Corporation. He shugged his shoulders in an attempt to lighten his thoughts. The watchful eyes of the dusty windows held a menacing quality, as if the whole place seemed to be waiting for him to make some wrong move, when the retaliation would be swift and decisive.

Pushing his way through the glass-panelled doors, he went inside. Now, he walked even more carefully than before, eyes watchful and alert. But the air of menace which he had felt outside, had disappeared now. A slender, good-looking woman was seated behind a desk at the end of the short entrance. She glanced up inquiringly as he walked forward, brows lifted slightly, her full lips close together as she eyed him appraisingly.

There was a cream telephone at her right hand, a typewriter in front of her and a shorthand pad close beside her from which she had obviously been typing her notes. At her back, a row of green, metal filing cabinets gave the place an air of respectability. If this was a front to a Communist-dominated organisation, they had certainly spared no trouble to make it seem authentic.

The woman smiled at him politely. 'Is there anything I can do for you?' she inquired.

Carradine answered her fluently: 'I came to see if there was any chance of getting a job with the Corporation.' He went on encouragingly: 'I'm a mining engineer by profession, but I'm quite willing to take on any other kind of job.'

'I doubt if we have any work available at the moment, Senor — ?'

'Perez. Miguel Perez.'

'Senor Perez, but if you'll take a seat, I'll inquire for you.'

'*Gracias.*' Carradine moved way, took a chair. The girl picked up the receiver, pressed a button on the desk in front of her and spoke rapidly into the telephone, her voice lowered, deliberately it seemed to Carradine, so that he could hear nothing of what she said. Someone at the other end of the line must have given her certain instructions, for as she replaced the receiver in its cradle she smiled broadly, said: 'Senor Cleron will see you now. Will you come this way?' She crossed the wide entrance to a door made of carefully blended panels of polished wood and pushed it open for him to go through. There was a dead silence in the room once the door had been closed behind him. Carradine felt it at once. It was not the normal quietness one found in an office such as this, it was the muffling stillness of a room which had been specially soundproofed.

He gave no outward sign that he had noticed anything unusual, stood patiently while the man seated behind the desk looked him over with stony eyes. Carradine looked stolidly back at him. The other was of average height, but his thick-set body made him appear shorter than he really was. His head, set on a bull neck, was topped by a thatch of close-cropped hair and the eyes, set close together, were brown and bulged a little as if trying to thrust themselves from his head. There were circles under the eyes, the skin pouched and the mouth was thin-lipped and tight. Not removing his glance from Carradine, the other placed a cigarette between his lips on the left side of his mouth, flicked the American lighter with an abrupt gesture, then spoke around the cigarette in a tight, clipped voice.

'What is your name?'

'Miguel Perez, Senor.'

'And you say that you are a mining engineer?' The other's gaze was flat and incurious. Evidently, thought Carradine, he had been listening in to the conversation in the outer room. These people certainly did not seem to miss a trick.

He nodded. 'Si, Senor. Unfortunately it is not easy to find work now and — '

'I am not interested in your personal problems, Perez,' said the other, smiling thinly. 'At the same time, the Aroyo Mining Corporation has entered on a policy of expansion and we do need labour to continue our work. Our organisation is widespread throughout South America and if you are engaged to work for us I can give no guarantee that it will be either as a mining engineer or in

Uruguay. Have I made myself understood?'

'Perfectly, Senor.' Carradine's face showed no emotion. He felt a little tingle run along his spine. There was little reason now to doubt the truth of what Merton had discovered about this place or the organisation behind it. This man was no Uruguayan. His country of origin lay somewhere behind the Iron Curtain, although he spoke the language with only a barely perceptible trace of accent.

The other went on in his softest voice: 'Naturally, we do not engage anyone without a thorough and complete investigation. You will give all necessary details to the secretary in the outer office. Each one of these will be checked within the next two hours. At the end of that time, you will return here. You will then be told whether or not we are able to use you.'

Carradine said nothing. It was, for the present, the end of the interview. Turning, he went out of the room. The girl behind the desk in the outer office glanced up, motioned him to sit down in the chair in front of her, pulled a long, printed form towards her, a pen in her right hand.

Now was the time for the questioning, Carradine thought tightly, as he lowered his body into the chair and settled himself comfortably. He could only hope that the background which had been provided for him by London, for use in an emergency such as this, would stand the probing it would receive from these people. It could not have been easy to set up a complete past life which would check out in every detail.

★ ★ ★

It was exactly six o'clock that evening when Carradine returned to the offices of the Aroyo Mining Corporation. This time, he was shown directly into the inner room. The squat man drew his lips back from his teeth. An inch of grey ash fell from the end of his cigarette into the silver tray. Expressionless eyes stared at Carradine as he stood in the middle of the room, hands hanging loosely by his sides. It was impossible to tell anything from the other's face. Had there been some slight mistake in the highly detailed past which had been set up for him? Some small seemingly insignificant point overlooked by the men whose job it had been to provide him with a name, a family, a career in mining technology at one of the universities. His fingers curled a little, ready to reach for the knife placed carefully along his wrist. The muscles of his stomach and chest felt tight under his flesh. Then the other pulled the printed sheet of paper in front of him, gave it a brief, cursory glance and tossed it on one side as if it were of no further use to him.

'You are prepared to work outside Uruguay?' The voice was a snap of clipped syllables.

'Of course.' Carradine nodded his head as casually as he could. 'Anywhere.'

'Very well. Everything has been arranged. Transport will be provided to take you, and seven others to the site. Once you arrive there, you may find things a little different from what you expect. You will, however, carry out orders. That is important if you wish to remain working for us.'

Was there a definite threat underlying the last words? A hint, veiled perhaps, but still recognisable, that unless he did as he was told, he would be killed? Carradine smiled inwardly. At least, his Uruguayan background must have checked out for these people and the first hurdle had been successfully passed. From this moment on, he would have to play this mission as he went along.

The other scribbled something on a piece of paper, pushed it across the desk to him. 'Be at this address in two hours' time. See that you are punctual.'

'I understand, senor.' Carradine took the paper and slipped it into the pocket of his jacket. 'I will be there.'

Carradine went out into the empty street, stood in the growing shadows at the corner for a while, keeping an unobtrusive eye on the red-brick building in the distance, but during the whole of that time, no one went in and nobody came out. He wondered what might be going on behind that seemingly innocent facade at that very moment. That squat man who was so obviously a Russian or a member of one of the countries of the Far Eastern Block — was he getting in touch with his colleagues by radio transmitter, informing them that a further batch of workers was due to arrive, sending details of every man so that there might be no slip-ups on the way? Might he be even checking further into Carradine's story, seeking some tiny piece of information which did not quite tie in? Getting tired of waiting, knowing that he might also attract unwelcome attention, he made his way along one of the streets which radiated from the small plaza there and found a tiny, cheap restaurant where he ordered a meal, some inexpensive wine and settled back in the seat near the window, chewing his food thoughtfully as he watched the early night crowds outside. The sun was going down now, almost on the horizon, hidden behind the looming blocks of the buildings on the other side of the street, but it still made its presence felt by the deep crimson glow which now spread to almost every part of the sky. The few clouds that were visible were touched by it, like smears of blood painted on some strange canvas by a surrealist painter.

The clouds broke up, the sky quickly lost its crimson hue and darkness began to settle over the city as he finished his meal, drained the last of the wine, feeling the warm, expanding glow in his stomach. He lit a cigarette, drew the smoke deep into his lungs, tried to get his thoughts into some form of order in his mind. The last time he had been in Montevideo, he had been a freelance photographer. There had been little danger attached to that job, a slight brush with the police perhaps who always, in these countries, seemed to find a delight in discovering fresh scenes which foreigners were not allowed to photograph for some obscure military reason.

Those had been carefree days. He smiled wryly to himself, stared down at the grey ash on the tip of the cigarette between his fingers as if he could find the answer to a lot of the questions which had been troubling him lately, there. What had made him change careers, enter the British Secret Service, give up that life of ease for one of danger and intrigue? A spirit of high adventure? The desire to help his country? The urge to do something different? Maybe even the glamour which was generally supposed to be associated with the life of a Secret Service agent?

With an effort, he put the thoughts of a dead youth from his mind, knowing that at the present moment they would only serve to clutter up his mind with a lot of useless information, at a time when he needed to be able to think clearly, quickly and decisively. Crushing out the butt of the cigarette, he pushed back his chair, rose to his feet and left the restaurant. Lights came on in some of the buildings. Far away, there was the dismal hooting of ships in the harbour. A couple of large trucks started up and growled along the street, heading out of the city. He checked the cheap watch on his wrist. He had another thirty-seven minutes left before reaching the address on the paper which had been given to him. Taking the paper out of his pocket, he checked the address. His brows lifted a little. It was somewhere on the northern outskirts of Montevideo. Obviously they would have chosen a place like this, out of the way, where there was little chance of them being interrupted.

Brushing his hands down his clothes, he began to walk north, thinking ahead, digging into his memory of the city, to work out in his mind the quickest route to his destination.

★　★　★

Carradine made his way swiftly through the quiet, shadowed streets on the outskirts of Montevideo, past low-roofed buildings that lifted to the full face of the moon, past long, oblong warehouses which had been empty for years, and finally along a maze of mean-looking streets that smelled of garbage, of the day's heat trapped between the houses. The last light of the day had gone. Under the dark indigo sky, lit in the east by the round yellow moon, he came out into open country, was conscious of a momentary feeling of doubt. Was this a trap? Had he been given the wrong address? There was nothing here but open grassland, stretching away into the darkness as far as he could see.

Now he walked even more carefully, cat-like, putting one foot in front of the other. The moon shone palely down on the scene in front of him. Three minutes later, he made out the dark shadow against the background of pampas grass. His breath eased from between his teeth. This was more like it. That long building could serve as a hangar. The ground beyond it was almost perfectly flat, held a lighter sheen in the moonlight than the rest. As he neared the building, he saw that he had not been mistaken. The silhouette of the plane was clearly visible in front of the hangar. The clean-cut lines of a Douglas DC-3. There was no mistaking it, even in the moonlit darkness.

As he made his way forward over the rough, coarse grass, Carradine examined everything. There were glimpses of a huddle of low, smallish buildings about half a mile away and a windsock that stood out stiffly in the freshening breeze.

A small, but he guessed legitimate, airfield, used exclusively for the Aroyo Mining Corporation. An excellent means of getting their men from one spot to another anywhere in South America. It could also be a good way of contacting a Soviet fishing vessel far out in the Atlantic, or maybe even a submarine. They had, at times, been reported from as far south as this.

There was a small group of men working around the plane and another group just visible inside the hangar. As he walked forward, one of the men detached himself from the group inside the hangar.

'You are the last of our passengers, Senor Perez,' said the man from the office in Montevideo. 'But you are punctual. We leave in five minutes.' He gestured to Carradine to join the others.

Outside, the propellers on the DC-3 began to spin, slowly at first, with a spluttering cough from the engines, then more quickly and the low hum rose to a shriller, raw-edged whine that grated on his ears. He gave his companions a quick look. All were of the usual peasant type, found in the old quarter of Montevideo, men who were prepared to take any kind of work so long as it paid well. The Reds must have engaged hundreds such men in the past couple of years, getting them out of the country by air. None of the men spoke. They seemed a little fearful of what lay ahead of them. Perhaps none of them had ever flown before and it would be a terrifying experience for them.

In the dimness, he smiled a little to himself. At least, he had a very definite advantage there. Most of his life during the past five years seemed to have been spent in some aircraft or another.

The thunderous roar of the engines came at him as he made his way towards the waiting plane. This type of aircraft had seen much use during the early years of the war, mainly as a troopcarrier. There were very few of them left in service now, but they were sturdy aircraft, well-built, and although this one shook and rattled in every rivet and seam, he did not doubt that it would get them to their destination in one piece.

Many of the interior fittings had been

stripped out of the plane, thereby giving it additional speed. With these special modifications, Carradine reckoned the DC-3 could possibly reach a maximum speed of over three hundred miles an hour. The hum of the engines arose to a harsh whine, the fuselage vibrated even more as the pilot fed power to the engines. Pressing his shoulders against the metal framework at his back, Carradine forced himself to relax. His fellow passengers sat stiffly on the twin steel benches which ran along either side of the interior. Their faces bore some sign of the strain they were experiencing. A man came through from the pilot's cabin and passed down the length of the plane, walking steadily in spite of the fact that they were now moving away from the hangar, rolling forward towards the end of the runway. Carradine thrust his head back further against the cold, shaking metal, turning his face away from the nearest light so that the shadow fell on to it. It was the man who had been seated in front of him on the flight from London to Montevideo!

Bits of the jigsaw puzzle began to slot themselves into place in his mind now. He had been shadowed all the way from London. These people never missed a trick. For the first time, he felt aware of the enormity of the organisation he was up against. He felt as if he were sitting on top of a smoking volcano, waiting tensely for it to erupt beneath him and blow him clear to Kingdom Come.

The man had glanced at him without curiosity as he had moved past, more intent on steadying himself than examining the faces of the passengers on this trip. Settling back, Carradine felt the plane gather speed. Its progress was bumpy over the uneven ground, then there was a sudden change; the heaving, shuddering motion ceased and he knew they were airborne. He let his pent-up breath go in little pinches through his nostrils. The DC-3 gathered itself and soared up into the dark sky in a smooth, easy climb.

Turning his head, Carradine glanced out of the small, square window close beside him. He was looking out into utter

158

blackness. He could just make out the smooth sweep of the aircraft's wing and the single engine on that side, the spinning propeller invisible, except on rare occasions when the moonlight touched the whirring arc with a faintly glistening sheen. They climbed higher and clouds began to gather beneath them now, solid-looking tufts of cloud, gleaming with the white moonlight, forming a sea of billowing cottonwool that looked so thick and solid it seemed impossible they could ever make their way back down through it again.

There was no talking among the rest of the men, spread out on the benches. The plane throbbed on, high above the weather, above the wind for the moment, the engines roaring loudly in their ears. The lights inside the aircraft had been turned low and Carradine sat in the cool darkness, legs thrust out straight in front of him, outwardly calm, inwardly his mind a seething turmoil.

He was on his own now; would be forced to make snap decisions. He —

There came a sudden, stomach-heaving

lurch. The plane seemed to drop like a stone for perhaps thirty feet. One of the men opposite Carradine yelled out, eyes wide with fear. He would have leapt to his feet had not one of the men next to him reached out and pulled him back. Another lurch, an ugly shrill whine as the pilot fed more power to the straining engines. Carradine turned his head instinctively. Outside, beyond the tiny window, the sky was suddenly darker than before. There was no moon-light and he saw to his surprise that they were flying in thick cloud that swirled and boiled around the plane, holding it in a tight-fisted embrace. There was a sudden vivid flash that seemed to fill the sky to its uttermost limits, a blue-bright glare which outlined the wing of the DC-3 in a weird halo of electric-purple light. Instinctively, Carradine drew back his head and a split second later, the crash of the thunder cracked against his ears, half deafening him. The plane leapt and bucked as if it had been struck by a giant hand. It seemed like the end of the world for everyone on board the plane. How the pilot was taking it, Carradine could not guess. Maybe he was used to these violent storms which could sweep up without warning across the flat, rolling plains of Argentina. There was the feel of danger in the air. Steve Carradine had felt it on too many occasions in the past not to be able to recognise it now. It was a real and tangible thing. A quivering of taut stomach muscles, a sudden ache pressure in the chest as if a network of small strings were being drawn tightly around the fast-beating heart. Again there was that ugly actinic glare of lightning outside the aircraft; a sickening bump, a violent tremor that ran throughout the whole length of the fuselage. How old were these DC-3s? he wondered. Nearly twenty years old perhaps. Long enough for the insidious fingers of metal fatigue to have penetrated the framework of the hull, wings and tail unit. There were forces at work in the heavens around them which could make a mockery of anything man could do. How could they hope to survive all of this?

He had faced danger and death many

times during his career, but it had always been something he could fight using whatever talents and weapons he possessed. But this was something different; something he could not fight, which had to be allowed to take its own course. This feeling of helplessness was the worst thing he had ever known.

There was a movement at the far end of the long passenger cabin. The door leading into the pilot's cabin slid open, a flood of yellow light streamed through into the dimness of the plane's interior. For a few moments, the shapes of two men were visible, engaged in deep conversation. Carradine watched them narrowly from beneath lowered lids, focusing his whole attention on them. He recognised both of them. His acquaintance of the flight from London and the man who had hired him in Montevideo. For a moment he felt the cold clamminess of sweat on his face as he saw them both lift their heads and peer in his direction. The short, squat man said something in a low undertone, then stepped forward, threaded his way between the rows of sprawled men until he halted directly in front of Carradine. He stood with his legs braced well apart, swaying easily to every violent movement of the aircraft. Carradine lifted his eyes and stared straight at him, wondering what was going on in the man's mind, whether there had been any recognition of him through his disguise.

Relaxing a little, the other said: 'You are a mining engineer, *mon amigo*. I do not doubt that you are a little above these other — peasants. They have no imagination at all.'

Carradine said nothing, as the other seated himself beside him. Did the other intend to tell him something of the work which was going on at the secret launching site — knowing that as an engineer, it would not take him long to realise what was happening there, that it was no ordinary mining operation which was being carried out?

The other's next words confirmed this. 'Now that we are on our way, and there is no possibility of turning back for any of you, perhaps it might help if you were to understand a little of what we are doing.'

Carradine shrugged. 'I gathered that you were a mining corporation. Is it prospecting for a new field?' His tone was casual. His face betrayed nothing.

The other uttered a short, sharp bark of a laugh which was almost drowned by the fearsome crash of thunder which enveloped the plane, slammed down against it from all sides.

'You might call it that, *amigo*. A new field. But not in the way you understand it.' He made himself more comfortable on the seat. 'You must have realised by now that neither my colleagues nor myself are natives of your country.' His lifted brows gave an interrogatory note to the statement.

Carradine gave a faint nod. 'A lot of the experts in Uruguay are foreigners,' he answered non-committally.

'Of course.' The other gazed away from Carradine, letting his glance slide over the faces of the other men. Then he said in a lower voice than before. 'As I said before, you are an intelligent man. When we arrive at our destination, you will see that what we are building is like nothing you have ever seen before.'

Carradine put just the right amount of surprise into his expression. 'But your office in Montevideo said — '

'The sign outside the door said just what we wanted it to say, nothing more,' said the other in a relaxed, conversational tone. 'You can help us with your engineering knowledge and there will be plenty of pesos in it for you. I'm sure you will not wish to turn down an offer like that.'

Carradine looked gravely down at the floor of the plane under his feet. 'I have no objection to being paid well for any kind of work. Business hasn't been too brisk for me during the past year or so.'

'That is as I guessed,' nodded the other. 'Briefly we are building a site for the launching of atomic warheaded missiles which can be brought to bear on any country of the Western Alliance within minutes. It will effectively alter the balance of power in this part of the world, adding to our strength here and nullifying the power of the United States.'

'I think I'm beginning to understand,' Carradine said seriously. 'And this work will all be top secret, of course.'

'Naturally.' The other gave him a bright-sharp stare. 'You must realise that we are doing it all for the good of your country, and the other states of South America. At present, you have no nuclear weapons with which to defend yourselves and we feel that it is only right that you should have some voice in any decision which may be taken at — perhaps, a Summit Meeting — when matters relating to you are discussed.'

Naturally, thought Carradine dryly. This was the propaganda, the half-lies of patriotism was one of the words they bandied about whenever they had the opportunity. Knowing the fiery tempers and the idealistic outlook of these Latin peoples, they must feel that they were on quite an easy wicket talking in this way, making them feel that by working with the Soviets, they were making *their* country, one of the most powerful in this part of the world. There had always been this feeling of suspicion on the part of the smaller countries of the American bloc against the United States. Maybe it was because America was *too* big, too powerful and influential in world matters. Nobody really liked playing the part of little brother, any more than they like being considered an insignificant country, backward and illiterate.

'Why are you telling me all this?' Very softly, Carradine matched the other's tone. 'I was engaged as a mining engineer. What if I should decide to go to the authorities and warn them of this — venture — of yours?'

'You wouldn't do that,' said the other flatly. His eyes pierced Carradine's skull, the level gaze going right through the back of his head.

'How can you be so sure? Either I do as I'm told or I don't get paid, is that it?'

The man smiled, showing his teeth. 'Either you do as you're told or you get killed. It is as simple as that. At the site, you will find yourself many miles from the nearest outpost of civilisation, cut off from the outside world by impenetrable jungle. Should you decide to try to get away, I assure you that you would not get very far, even if you managed to slip past the guards. We also have ways of learning about escapes before they actually happen and our methods of punishment might not appeal to a man of your intellect and imagination.' His voice sent a little shudder up and down Carradine's spine. The man, he knew, was utterly evil.

He nodded. 'I am beginning to understand what I've let myself in for,' he said without emotion. 'And the rest of these men? Will you be holding them by the same kind of threat?'

'That is often not necessary. We pay them well, far more than they could get anywhere else in this country. They do not stop to consider what they are doing so long as there are plenty of pesos for them to send home.'

Carradine leaned back in his seat. Outwardly, he seemed to be turning over the position in his mind, brow furrowed in thought. Inwardly, he was preparing his mind for what would come once they arrived at their destination. On purpose, he had made this man feel that he might question some of the things he found so that their respect for him might be increased and their view of him — as a man who might be useful to them once they discovered that he could be trusted — would be confirmed. A lot was going to depend on how well he could convince them that he was ready to throw in his lot with them, for a price. Obviously they would need men who could supervise the others, could be placed in positions of trust, and it would be men such as these who would have the opportunity of learning the most about this place. But he would have to be careful. It needed only one slight mistake and it could be the end of the game for him.

'Think over what I've told you,' said the other softly. He got to his feet, then bent so that his mouth was close to Carradine's ear. 'But don't breathe a word of our little conversation to anyone else, otherwise it could mean trouble.'

Carradine said nothing, but continued to stare after the other as he made his way back to the pilot's compartment. For a moment, ten seconds perhaps, certainly not longer, the man stood in the opening at the end of the plane, staring back at Carradine. Then he lowered the curtain, went through into the control cabin and closed the door behind him.

Slowly, Carradine turned his glance towards the man seated next to him. The other did not seem to have heard a word of the conversation. If he had, there was no interest on his face. Outside the aircraft, the storm was abating swiftly. They had flown through the worst part of it while he had been in conversation with the Russian. Strange that the mere act of talking could often force the mind away from even the greatest feeling of terror. Now there were the usual noises of the plane. The pounding, insistent roar of the twin engines, the faintly heard shriek of air past the airframe, the shaking, shuddering vibration of metal as it quivered in tune to the throbbing motors. The round, spectral eye on the moon appeared as the plane banked to port. The clouds drifted away from in front of it and it sailed out into a wide, clear patch of sky, almost, it seemed, on a level with them. They were probably flying around eight thousand feet now, he reckoned. Down below, there could be the pampas, or thick jungle, it was impossible to tell which. Even where there was no cloud, the ground was a dark carpet of midnight, featureless, without even a hint as to its composition.

He sat quietly in the dimness, letting himself relax. After a while, he closed his eyes, head resting uncomfortably against the chill metal at his back. Presently, he was asleep while the DC-3 flew on through the night.

Four hundred and fifty miles from its point of take-off, the plane swung north after travelling almost due west for most of the night. Argentina had gone below them, now they were over the heart of the jungle, a dark and poisonous green which could just have been made out where the moonlight fell as a dull grey wash over the unbroken stretches of trees down beneath them, with occasionally a river shining like a strip of silver wire against the darker and more monotonous background.

Carradine woke with the change in the note of the engines as they began to lose height. He sat up with a sudden start and stared about him. Nothing had changed. The interior of the plane was still as dim. Outside, the moon had altered its position in the sky, was much lower now, almost touching the distant horizon and it was just possible to make out the contours of the ground below them in the greying light of an early dawn. Here and there, a low hill lifted from the flatness of the terrain over which they were flying. Dense jungle lay everywhere with very few clearings to be seen. Where in God's name did the pilot intend to land this aircraft? Surely there couldn't be a stretch of open ground long enough or even level enough to take a plane this size.

His thoughts were interrupted by the appearance of one of the crew in the doorway. 'We shall be landing in ten minutes. Please remain seated after we touch down. Further orders will then be given to you.'

So they didn't intend any of them to get out and start looking around, thought

Carradine grimly. Evidently they had a lot to hide here. The plane hit an air pocket. Carradine's body jerked back with the sudden kick and his teeth were snapped shut in his head. He tried to sit calmly and relaxed. The jungle drifted below them as the DC-3 slid into its landing glide, lining up with the landing ground still some forty or fifty miles ahead, out of sight from where he sat. They were flying quite steadily now with the dawn brightening in the eastern half of the sky. The tops of the trees were a green blur beneath the wing. Here and there, he was able to pick out a wide, sluggish river that wound around the base of a rising hill. Once or twice, he saw a clearing in the rain forest. But in every direction, dominating the scene out to the far horizons there was only the jungle; dense, poisonous, deadly. The Russian's words came back to him as he stared down at it. Even if one got through the guards surrounding the launching site, the chances of getting through the jungle were infinitely remote, if not non-existent.

Glancing down at his hands, he saw

that they were quite steady. Sighing a little, he leaned back. The feeling of being on his own in this place, knowing that the slightest slip could mean the end of everything, disturbed him. How could one man hope to fight the organisation these people had built up over the past few years? The security system at this site would be quite fantastic. They would leave nothing to chance. And the fact that back in Montevideo, they had made more than one attempt to kill him, indicated quite clearly that they suspected someone would have been sent to track down the whereabouts of this launching site. Merton had been killed because he had certain knowledge; not as much as he, Carradine, possessed. But it had been sufficient for the M.G.B. to realise that he could be troublesome. For all he knew, this could be a complicated M.G.B. plot to get him out here, unsuspecting, to finish him in this desolate, out-of-the-way spot, where nobody would be any the wiser. Back in London, they might be able to trace his progress part of the way and then come up against a brick wall.

Another agent might be assigned to this job and it was possible he would stumble on the Aroyo Mining Corporation and discover that they were merely a front for the Reds.

The day outside brightened. The sun popped up over the eastern horizon, springing up redly into the clear heavens. They were still three or four thousand feet up and the ground immediately below them still lay in darkness. Leaning as far back as he could, pressing the side of his face close to the cold perspex of the window, he tried to make out the terrain in front of them. They were banking in a wide sweep now, the screech of air past the plane sounding above the throttled back whine of the engines. A few moments later, he made out the vast space which had been gouged out of the jungle. The bare tract of ground stood out like a scar on the surface of the countryside. While the aircraft executed a wide curve, Carradine watched the ground below, searching for his first sight of any of the installations. He was doomed to disappointment. He could see nothing beyond a few wooden buildings and a larger, concrete erection which stood a little way to one side of the landing strip. The plane came out of its banking turn and the scene vanished. He could see nothing but the jungle trees now, reaching up for the belly of the plane as it sped over them. They were losing height rapidly, levelling off as they approached the runway.

Wedging himself tightly against the fuselage, he braced his back against the hard metal and waited for touch-down. There was a bump that sent a shudder through the plane, a rattling of metal, then a high-screeched wail for several seconds as the pilot cut the engines. The wheels hit the ground for a second time, then they were down, rolling towards the far end of the airstrip. He let his breath go in a harsh exhalation, realised that he was trembling a little.

They came to a halt in front of the concrete building. Carradine eyed it curiously through the window while they waited for orders to disembark. Merely a control tower of some kind, he decided finally. Clearly it was nothing to do with the launching site. He tried to see beyond it, all the way across the cleared section, but there was nothing visible. Had he been mistaken? Were the builders so far behind schedule that they had not erected any of the installations yet? Or had they been brought to the wrong place, brought here for further questioning before allowed to proceed with the rest of the journey?

A host of ideas tumbled through his mind, were halted as the harsh voice from the pilot's cabin shouted. 'Outside everybody!'

Carradine pushed himself stiffly to his feet. His right leg had lost all feeling due to the cramped position in which he had been forced to sit. He limped slowly after the others, down the short flight of steps which had been thrust up against the side of the plane, out into the first, red rays of the morning sun. The air was still crisp and cold and he felt it bite at his throat and lungs as he drew down a deep breath. But it cleared his head and he looked about him with some curiosity.

'You will first be taken to your quarters,' said the squat, broad-shouldered Russian. 'Then you will be told where to begin work.'

They began to move off. Now that they were off the plane, the rest of the passengers seemed to have perked up, become more interested in their surroundings. As Carradine stepped forward, to fall in with the rest, the squat man laid a hand on his arm. 'You will come with me, Senor Perez,' he said authoritatively. 'Those men are simply workers. We have something a little different for you.'

Again there was that faint tremor in his arms and legs as he followed the other over the rough ground, past the concrete control block, across a boulder-strewn patch of ground towards the rising slope of the hillside in the distance. The man beside him was silent and Carradine knew better than to ask any questions, even though there were a hundred of them in his mind, each demanding an answer. Patience and watchfulness were required now if he was not to give himself away. Very soon, within the next few minutes perhaps, he would know whether he had fooled these men or not, whether he would go on living with a chance to disrupt their plans and find out how the nuclear warheads were to be brought here, or whether they had their own plans for him.

Carradine's companion walked directly towards the jungle trees, where they had not been cleared. Curious, he followed close on the man's heels. A dank smell, mixed with a faint animal stench greeted them as they walked into the undergrowth. There was a narrow path here that wound among the trees. Picking his way carefully forward, he noticed the glimmer of steel among the thick foliage. They came upon the mouth of the tunnel almost unexpectedly. It led, he guessed, right into the hillside and was excellently hidden from the air. He doubted if any plane ever flew over this stretch of the country, yet these people had spent thousands, possibly millions of pesos, building everything underground.

Perhaps they were looking to the future when the U.S. spy satellites were in orbit, photographing every square mile of ground, relaying back all of the relevant data to their control centres. There might be danger of discovery then and the Russians had been clever enough to have foreseen it.

The tunnel went on downwards and would, he guessed, go right below the surface of the hill, perhaps a mile underground. Lights gleamed at intervals along the curved walls and a set of glittering rails ran down the centre of the tunnel which was more than thirty feet in diameter. It was a tremendous achievement, but there was more to come.

The man beside him said suddenly: 'It is a long walk. Fortunately all of it is down hill.' His short, sharp laugh was thrown back at them by the curved walls. 'An engineer such as yourself will be able to appreciate the immensity of an undertaking such as this. I am neither a scientist nor an engineer. My job is security. But even I cannot fail to be — how would you say it, exhilarated

— by all of this.'

Fifty yards along the tunnel, it widened and then branched into three, each more brilliantly lit than the single tunnel from the surface. His guide took the one on the left, their footsteps echoing hollowly from the walls and the roof which curved over their heads. In the distance, there was a heavy, rhythmic beat of machinery, like a great mechanical heart beating amid the complex array of tunnels. They were approaching the nerve centre of the huge installation.

Three minutes later, the tunnel opened out into a vast underground chamber which had been hewn out of the solid rock. It was larger than he had expected, perhaps five hundred yards in length and about three hundred in width. The roof was perhaps a hundred feet above his head, blazing with lights. As he stepped through, into the chamber, he noticed the edges of the steel doors which formed the end of the tunnel, doors which could, he knew, be closed at a moment's notice. A little prickle of apprehensive wonder touched his spine. He knew now why they had been so worried about this place back in London, why Merton had been killed so that his information might die with him.

6

A Web of Shadows

'These will be your living quarters while you are working here.' The squat man whose name, Carradine had learned, was Donovsky, stood in the doorway of the small room and waved an expressive hand to indicate the amenities. The room was more like a cell than anything Carradine had seen before. A wash basin in one corner, an iron bed, a small chest of drawers and a couple of chairs made up the meagre furniture. There was a solitary carpet on the concrete floor with a flower pattern on it. Carradine felt a twinge of grim amusement. Evidently, as one of the engineers on the project, they reckoned he rated some form of luxury.

'Thank you.' He gave a brief nod. One thing, there was plenty of light in the room. He guessed that there were several powerful dynamos supplying them with all of the electrical power they needed.

'You will be given instructions concerning your work here in a little while. In the meantime, you must remain in your quarters. Failure to observe this rule could lead to trouble.'

There was no mistaking the menace in the other's tone. Carradine nodded again, settled himself in one of the chairs as the other closed the door. On an instinct, he went over to the door and turned the knob slowly. As he had guessed, the door was locked. Nothing for it now but to make the best of things, he decided. He thought of his room at the Hotel Uruguayo, for a moment his thoughts slipped back to the girl, Valentina Veronova, tall and beautiful, deadly perhaps, but still fun to be with; and suddenly he found himself wishing that he was back there instead of here in this sterile room, devoid of any of the material comforts. He had a momentary impression of men scurrying around underground here like ants in some gigantic anthill and the thought chilled him, although he was not sure why. There were a couple of mining journals on the top of the bureau. He took them down and riffled through them, studying their contents. He knew very little about mining, but he doubted if anyone would go into it in great detail unless they already suspected him and were wanting to catch him out. The engineering required for a site such as this would be far more complex and specialised than anything an ordinary mining engineer would be supposed to know and he had the feeling that if they wanted him to help in the work here, he would be put under the wing of someone already at work on the site. When that happened, it would be up to him to keep his eyes and ears open, to discover all he could about this place and particularly where any secret plans were kept and how the nuclear warheads were to be smuggled into the country, ready for the missiles which he knew to be already there.

Even if he was successful on either of these two counts, what would there be for him to do? He made up his mind on that at once. Somehow, he would have to get out of this place, even if it meant trying to steal the plane. How much that would achieve, he wasn't sure apart from alerting the organisation as to his true identity. Would he be able to get the information back to London or the FBI? If so, would they be able to stop those nuclear warheads from being brought into the country? The last thing America would want would be an international incident. Everything would have to be done discreetly and with the maximum amount of security and secrecy. He stared down at the magazine in his hands, listened to the far away hum of machinery and tried to calm his jumping nerves and clear his mind of the background thoughts which persisted in cluttering it up, making it difficult to think things out clearly.

An hour passed; an hour during which nothing happened. During that time, Carradine's imagination ran riot as he tried to figure out what might be happening outside that steel door which had been so unceremoniously locked on him. It was possible that he had been recognised on the plane by his fellow-traveller from London, who could only have been some high-ranking man from Moscow. It was equally likely that they had discovered something when they had checked out his background in Montevideo, maybe even connecting him with Merton. Were these men, even now, working out how best to dispose of him, starting more inquiries into his past, sending word back to Montevideo, asking for more information about Perez, a man who called himself an engineer?

The door opened, shutting off his train of thought. Donovsky stood in the opening. He said shortly: 'They are waiting for you now, Perez. Come with me and I'll take you to them.'

Carradine had expected a brief smile from the other, but there was nothing. The thick lips twisted just a little and the cold eyes regarded him with the stillness of a snake watching its prey just before it struck. Donovsky stood on one side to allow Carradine to precede him, snapped off the light switch before closing the door and falling into step beside him.

Carradine looked up into the other's square features. He knew the type well enough, had met up with men like this on past missions. Dedicated men, knowing only one purpose, to carry out any orders given them and see that things ran smoothly, answering directly to Moscow if anything went wrong. While in Moscow, he would perform routine jobs, see to despatches, check reports coming in from all over the world. At intervals, he would be given assignments such as this, missions which were given only to men who could be trusted implicitly, for there had been too many occasions in the past when agents whom the Soviets had considered to be reliable, had sought, and been given, political asylum. They had brought certain secrets with them which had made their going over to the other side even more of a defeat for the M.G.B. than might ordinarily have been the case.

The man's eyes were hard and flinty, as they were in most of the men who worked outside of Russia. They knew that they were under observation every minute of the time, their actions watched closely and noted, every detail about them filed away somewhere for future reference and if there was the slightest failure associated with their work, they could expect immediate recall to Russia, with its attendant punishment. All of this went through Carradine's mind as he glanced up at Donovsky.

As if feeling his glance on him, the other turned his head sharply, drew back his lips and said thinly: 'You may not find the work here to your liking, Senor Perez. It will be a little more specialised than any which you have carried out in the past. However, the rewards of success are great and we are almost nearing completion of the major project.'

Was there a hint of defensiveness in the other's tone? Perhaps he had found out that all of the credentials given for Perez had checked and the higher powers here had decreed that he was to be treated with a certain amount of deference according to his status. Carradine was not aware how highly he had been rated by the men in London whose job it had been to provide him with a background which would stand up to expert probing. He knew they would have done their best to give him such a professional background as to afford him as much freedom as possible on this site, always assuming that the Reds were prepared to treat scientific men in such a way that those who were able to give them the most help could expect certain privileges. Since there was no way off the site for any of the workers or scientific men recruited from the South American countries, until the project was completed and the Reds were sure that it was safe for them to disclose the whereabouts of the launching site, there was a strong possibility that they might be a little more lax with their information than otherwise.

'I think I've seen enough already to tell me that whatever it is you are building, it's something on a very large scale. Evidently, since virtually everything is underground, where it cannot be seen from the air, this is a project you do not wish others to know of. Am I right?'

'Certainly. It is as well if the world at large knows nothing of this until we are in a position to tell them.'

'Then from that I gather it has a tremendous military value. I can think of no other reason for going to all of this expense and trouble.' Carradine felt on safe ground talking to the other in this way. Had he tried to pretend that he knew nothing of what was happening here, above what had been told him on the plane coming across from Montevideo, it would have increased the other's suspicions of him.

Donovsky nodded. 'Obviously you have a great many questions to ask and although I can answer many of them, they will be answered by Lieutenant-General Vozdashevsky, the Head of Operations here.'

Carradine allowed himself a quick lift of his eyebrows. To Donovsky, the expression of surprise would be because of the mention of such a high-ranking officer at this lonely place. The truth was that the surprise in Carradine's mind came from the mention of the name, not the rank of the man who was Head of Operations here. Vozdashevsky! Here was a man close to the top in Moscow, in charge of everything here. If he had needed it, this was sufficient testimony to the importance which Moscow placed on this project. He knew quite a lot of Vozdashevsky's background, although he had never met the man face to face. He did not know of any British agent who had. Now it seemed, he was to be accorded that doubtful privilege.

Donovsky led him along a short passage which evidently connected two of the long tunnels he had seen earlier. A steel door in the side of the passage was partly open and through it, he had a glimpse of the long operations room which he had seen before being escorted to his quarters. There was still plenty of activity in evidence.

Donovsky paused in front of a section of the passage, thumbed a concealed switch. A smooth metal section slid noiselessly to one side. Donovsky's face was still and impassive as he motioned Carradine inside. Stepping through, he found himself in a well-appointed office. The highly-polished desk gleamed in the diffuse light which came from a trio of overhead lamps, set close to the ceiling. Behind the desk, sat Lieutenant-General Vozdashevsky. Carradine felt his mouth go dry for a second, and the muscles of his jaw stood out under the skin as he stared across at the other. The completely bald head shone in the light, the forehead so high that the skull appeared to be domed. The lower lip was thrust out in an almost petulant expression and the cold eyes looked stolidly at Carradine as he advanced towards the desk.

Vozdashevsky placed the tips of his long, tapered fingers together and eyed him over the pryramid formed. The nails were immaculately cut and polished and everything about him suggested a man who prided himself in his outward appearance. His face was hard and unyielding, the face of a man accustomed to giving orders and having them carried out without question. A very dangerous man indeed.

'Do you wish to smoke, Senor Perez?' The other spoke politely, the accent very pronounced. He pushed a packet of cigarettes across the top of the polished desk.

'Thank you.' Carradine took one, leaned forward as the other flicked a lighter and applied the flame to the end of the cigarette. He drew the smoke down into his lungs as he straightened up. Not once did the other remove his gaze from his face, the eyes unblinking.

'You will forgive me if I smoke one of my own,' said the other, leaning back in his chair. 'I have never been able to accustom myself to the Western type of cigarettes. I prefer the *papyrossi*.' As he spoke, he opened a small packet and took out the long slender cardboard tube of the Russian type of cigarette, squeezed it between his fingers a little, then inserted it in his mouth and lit it with a flourish. 'Please sit down, Senor Perez.' He indicated the chair which had been placed conveniently a little to one side of the desk. As he lowered himself into it, Carradine noticed that he was in direct line of the light from the lamp on the corner of the desk, the light shining into his eyes. If the other had noticed this, if it had been done deliberately, he gave no outward sign.

Donovsky had taken up his position close to the door, standing straight with his back to the wall. His flat eyes were fixed on Carradine's profile, almost as if he were trying to remember if he had ever seen him before. With an effort, Carradine put the uneasiness out of his mind, tried to concentrate on the man seated behind the desk. It seemed probable that every senior member of the staff here would be subjected to some form of interrogation such as this.

Although it was soon obvious that neither man intended to take any notes during this interview, but there would be a microphone hidden away somewhere and everything that was said would be recorded. The room had the impression that it had been wired for sound. There might even be a camera tucked away somewhere, focused on him, picking out every flicker of emotion, every show of expression, that flickered across his face.

'I understand that you are a mining engineer, Senor Perez. If that is so, then you may be extremely useful to us. Not, of course, that this is the type of work you are used to carrying out, but your knowledge of engineering could be of great help to us. In this project, we have been forced to bring several of our own technicians with us, but the more we can recruit from the neighbouring countries, the more quickly we will be able to complete our work. In addition to this, there will be the need to have men here permanently to maintain the installations.' He paused, delicately flicked the half-inch of grey ash from the tip of the *papyrossa*, then thrust it back between his lips once more. 'You will have realised the full significance of everything you have seen so far. We are building a launching site for intercontinental ballistic missiles which are already here and will soon be equipped with atomic warheads. Once that is done, we shall be in a position to challenge the United States in this area.'

Vozdashevsky paused to allow the full implications of his words to sink in. Glancing across the desk, he studied Carradine's face, watching closely for his reactions to the news.

'And the United States? What will their reaction be once they know of this?'

Vozdashevsky spread his hands in a meaningful gesture. He shrugged his shoulders slightly. 'By the time they know of this little project of ours, it will be too late for them to do anything, but accept the position as gracefully as possible. Naturally, they will not like it. But for some years now, we have been forced to accept American bases in Turkey, right on our very doorstep. There are other American and British bases all around the Soviet Union.' His face hardened and there was a brief glitter in his eyes. His voice had risen in pitch. Almost, thought Carradine with a faint inward sense of amusement, as if he had been delivering a speech to a full-dress meeting of the Praisidium.

As if he had suddenly realised the full melodrama of the situation, he lowered his voice as he went on. 'We have been working to a very strict schedule here and everything has gone as planned. The missiles themselves have been brought

197

into the country under the very noses of the American Navy and even now, they suspect nothing.'

Carradine allowed a little flicker of apprehension to cross his well-trained features. 'But you said they would be equipped with atomic warheads. Does that mean these are here, on the site?'

Vozdashevsky eyed him closely for a second. The fingers around the *papyrossa* tensed a little. Then he smiled, shrugging his shoulders. 'I see that you are a very clever man, Senor Perez. You do not like the idea of having nuclear weapons on the site where you are working?' His teeth flashed in the light as she smiled broadly.

Carradine gave a quick nod of his head. 'I have seen pictures of Hiroshima and Nagasaki,' he explained. 'They were terrible. If there should be an accident of any kind, it could mean — ' He broke off, giving the impression that the consequences of such a disaster were too terrible for his mind to contemplate.

'The possibility of any accident can be dismissed,' said Vozdashevsky quietly, positively. 'Our scientists have been working with these weapons for many years. They have learned how to handle them. They cannot explode unless they are primed and this will not be done unless the necessity arises in the future. At the moment, you may sleep soundly. The warheads are not yet on the site. Soon, they will arrive, but your work will not be connected with them in any way. Our own specialists will deal with them under conditions of top security. Your work will be confined to the maintenance of the equipment here and the site itself.'

'I understand.' Carradine flicked the ash from his cigarette. He felt an inward sense of relief at the news that the warheads had still not arrived. It gave him the chance to find out where they were at present and with luck, how they were to be got into the country. It stood to reason that they would not try to bring them openly into the country, and it would be virtually impossible to smuggle anything as intricate and large as a nuclear device through the Customs. Evidently they had some way of getting it here which they considered to be foolproof. He could not imagine them trying it, unless they were sure of success.

'I have studied your past history,' went on the other smoothly, tapping a long forefinger against the thin file in front of him. 'It makes very interesting reading. You belong to no political party, indeed you appear to have an aversion to all forms of politics. This has something to commend it. Whether or not you agree with our form of Communism, you seem to be a man with a feeling for his country and I'm sure that you want to see it take its real place in the world. For too long, the peoples of the South American states have been downtrodden by the capitalistic countries. They have been looked upon as the poor relations, poor both economically and scientifically. But with our help, that can all be changed and I feel sure that a man with your education and background will be one of the first to realise this. It is our intention to help countries such as yours, particularly militarily, in order that you might have more say in the councils of the world. Only this way, will you cease to be exploited.'

Carradine nodded, but said nothing, knowing that the other had more to say, that he would go on without any prompting.

'You will find that conditions here are austere. They could scarcely be otherwise, considering that we are more than fifty miles from the nearest outpost of civilisation and those fifty miles are covered by some of the densest jungle in the world. However, you will find that your quarters provide you with all of the necessities of life. During the next few weeks, while you are working here, you will be kept under constant surveillance. This may be irksome, but it is absolutely necessary. Perhaps later, you will be granted certain privileges. I should, at this point, warn you against trying to get away from here. Several men have been dissatisfied with conditions on the site and have tried to get away. None have succeeded. If you looked, you might find the remains of some of them in the jungle, not far from here. Others were shot by the guards. I tell you this, in case you should be tempted to emulate them. Believe me, it is not worth the risk.' The smile was back on his lips, but it was a death's-head grimace, with no warmth in it and the eyes held a look of warning which was clearly visible.

He slapped his palm on the top of the file in front of him. 'I'm sure you will be happy working with us, Senor Perez. That is all.'

Carradine paused, then got slowly to his feet, leaned forward and stubbed out the butt of the cigarette. Outside, in the corridor, he asked Donovsky, 'Does the Lieutenant-General see everyone before they start work here?'

'Only those who will occupy senior positions in the organisation,' said the other quietly. He turned and smiled almost pleasantly. 'Your file gives you as clean a bill of health as we can expect.' He hesitated, then went on as though speaking in great confidence. 'Those men the Lieutenant-General spoke of, who were shot by the guards. I would not think too much about them if I were you. They were fools. They did not stop to think what the consequence of their actions might be and that is the mark of a man who does not care whether he lives or dies. I have had experience in life and death. Sometimes, I have to give the orders which result in men being executed. It is not easy. Being an executioner can often result in a sickening for the work. It is my profession, to originate the chain of events which results in a man dying. Shall we say that I am like a surgeon. Whenever I see something which threatens a project such as this, it is my duty to cut it out, to eradicate it completely before it has a chance to spread. A surgeon often has to remove a particular organ, not so much because it is diseased, but because its presence in the body threatens the life of the patient. That is how I look on myself.'

For a moment, Carradine wondered why the other was telling him all of this, unburdening his feelings on to him in this way. Could it be that Donovsky was getting sick of murder, of slaughtering innocent men whose only desire was to leave this place? Or had the other some deeper, more sinister, motive for confiding in him? Maybe he considered that if Carradine was something different to what he seemed to be on the surface, the best way to find this out would be to worm his way into his confidence. He felt a little twinge of grim amusement. Even in Russia, he thought inwardly, whenever an executioner began to lose interest in his work, they soon found another man to do his job and the first thing this man did, was to execute the former executioner.

Donovsky took him into the large underground control room. Standing beside him, Carradine let his keen gaze wander unobtrusively over the work in progress there. Electricians were wiring the complex mechanisms along one side of the room, some were computers, electronic equipment which would guide the missiles as they were launched, taking control of the rockets from the moment they were readied for firing, down through the ticking seconds of count-down, to blast-off and then continuing to make the minute adjustments to their courses once they were in the air, heading for their distant targets. Delicate servo-mechanisms were in the final stages of completion. Other pieces of equipment, whose function he did not recognise, were in various stages of completion.

A tall, dark-haired man came over from one side of the room as Donovsky crooked a finger. There was a polite nod of greeting. 'You will work for the time being with Karafio. He will tell you everything you need to know. At the end of the working period, you will return to your quarters. Meals will be brought to you there.'

Turning on his heel, the other walked away without a backward glance. Carradine watched him go for a moment, then turned his attention to the man beside him.

Karafio said quietly. 'You will be one of the new men who came on the plane this morning.'

'That's right.' Carradine gave a quick jerk of his head. 'I asked for a job in Montevideo. I was under the impression that I would be working for the Aroyo

Mining Corporation, but this is something I hadn't bargained for, I'm afraid. I know very little about electronics.' He waved a hand towards the banks of instruments and computers.

The other laughed easily. 'Don't let this worry you too much. You will soon get used to them. They can be a little overpowering at first sight, but very soon, you will find yourself working with them as if you had been used to them all of your life.'

For the remainder of the day, Carradine stayed close to Karafio as the other explained the workings of the various instruments in the control chamber. Slowly, gradually, he was able to build up some sort of a picture of the place in his mind. As he listened to what little bits of information the other man could provide, he felt his skin begin to crawl as he realised the enormous potentialities of this place, situated as it was in this strategic spot. It was obvious that the Russians had been planning this for many years. How long, it was impossible to tell. Certainly as long as they had been in possession of nuclear arms themselves. They must have realised, during the very early years after the war, that to gain the upper hand in the cold war, it would be necessary to nullify British and American bases around the periphery of the Soviet Union, to site a launching station in the very backyard of the NATO countries. The mere existence of this base was sufficient evidence of how well they had succeeded.

No matter what happened to him personally, even if it meant his life, he would have to get word of this back to London or Washington, leave them to deal with it in any way they saw fit. Beyond that, he could do very little. One man could not pit himself against all of this. He wondered how much time he had to give that warning. Every day that passed would bring those nuclear warheads closer to the base. Once they arrived, it would make things difficult, if not impossible for the men in Washington to take the necessary action. If he could only discover how they were being brought, when and where they were due to arrive, and get that information back too, it would be the only means of destroying the warheads before they reached their destination.

That evening, in his quarters, he went over everything he had learned. It seemed precious little. Brusquely, he closed his mind to the thought of those atomic devices on their way there from Russia, and focused all of his attention instead, on the position as he found it there, in this vast underground site which had been kept such a secret project that it had only come to the ears of the British Secret Service in London as the merest whisper of suspicion.

★　★　★

It was a busy, confused three days which followed for Carradine. As time went on, he picked up more tiny bits of information and from the seemingly scattered pieces, filled in more and more of the jigsaw puzzle. The missiles, he learned, by asking apparently innocent questions, were housed in an underground chamber some distance removed from the control units. They would remain hidden beneath the hillside until needed, being launched from underground to provide greater protection both from possible enemy action and observation from the air. More than half of the men on the site were Russian technicians. They had built the prototype control units and computers and were now training the rest of the men employed there. How much of the nature of the work the Government knew, Carradine was unable to discover. Very little, it seemed. The generals might have been told something about it, but it would be a simple matter for the true nature of the project to be hidden from them in a welter of scientific jargon. One day, the Government and the Army would wake up and realise that there was a missile-launching site in their midst and by that time, it would be far too late to start asking questions, or to do anything about it.

The ordinary labourers were carefully segregated from the rest of the scientific staff and the minor psychological factors which usually went with a tremendous scheme such as this had all been foreseen and prepared for by Lieutenant-General Vozdashevsky and the security men under his command. It was certainly this man who had achieved this minor miracle. If they had not been on opposite sides of the fence, Carradine could have even felt some kind of grudging admiration for the man.

By the end of the fourth day, he had learned sufficient about the running of the site and its layout to be able to formulate a plan. A few questions here and there, combined with a little tactical eaves-dropping, had enabled him to discover that the nuclear warheads were being brought from Russia on board a submarine which was due to reach the west coast some time within the next five days. Vozdashevsky himself, would travel to the coast to rendezvous with the submarine and bring back the warheads. The coastline less than a hundred miles west of the site was apparently particularly suited to a night landing. Rugged and desolate, it would be a simple matter for the devices to be transferred from the submarine standing offshore, to a handful of trucks, ready to bring them back to the site.

The sheer simplicity and audacity of the plan made it all the more likely to succeed. Carradine lay back on the iron bed, stared up at the low ceiling, and forced himself to relax. There was a further piece of information which he had learned which could be of the greatest importance. Vozdashevsky kept all of his top secret papers in a safe inside one of the offices halfway along the tunnel leading to the surface. London would give their eyes to get their hands on those papers and with a little luck, it was possible he might be able to do just that before getting out of this place. He had already made up his mind that the only possible way of escape lay in stealing the DC-3. It was the only means of transport from the site which gave him any chance of getting far enough from the place in time to throw off all pursuit.

Lying there on his back, he turned everything over in his mind, weighing up the pros and cons of the situation as he saw them, assessing every possibility. Within the next twenty-four hours, he would have to check the position of every guard along the tunnel and particularly in the vicinity of the office containing the secret papers, and the plane which was apparently left close to the concrete control block, fuelled and ready for instant use. There were sure to be alarms inside that office, but that was a risk he would have to take if he wanted to lay hands on those papers. If he could quickly get rid of any guards there, he reckoned he would have fifteen minutes at the most in which to crack that safe and get away. Once he was in the air, nothing could stop him, unless they got in touch with the Argentinian Government and asked that he be shot down or forced down, accusing him of stealing the plane.

There were so many possibilities that it was difficult to assess the situation correctly. Behind all of his reasoning, he was forced to admit there was a lot of wishful thinking. He was on his own. There was no one here that he could trust to help him and the desire to face up to these people, single-handed, and defeat them, was almost overwhelming. It was only by a tremendous effort of will that he was able to force the feeling away, and think things out objectively in his mind.

★ ★ ★

There was only the one guard outside the office in the outer tunnel. Carradine gave him a seemingly cursory glance as he made his way past him the following morning; but that single glance had taken in everything, the manner in which the man paced for twenty feet or so in front of the door, for ten feet on either side, so that for half of the time, he had his back to the door he was supposedly guarding. In addition to this, there was a narrow passage which led off into the rock not more than forty feet from the office. It led to a storeroom and the lighting there was not as good as in the main corridors. A man could conceal himself there without being noticed. As for getting inside the office, he had already ascertained that

Vozdashevsky took any papers he had been working on during the day down to the safe at precisely nine o'clock each evening as regularly as clockwork and that the guard, once he had satisfied himself as to the identity of the other, continued with his rhythmic, monotonous pacing, taking no further interest in the Lieutenant-General. All that remained for Carradine to do, to put his plan into operation, was to ensure that the door of his quarters, which was of the self-locking type, was not locked that evening after the last meal of the day . . .

Carradine had eaten all of the food on the tray and was smoking one of his meagre supply of cigarettes when the door opened and the guard came in. The other looked relaxed and almost cheerful as he bent, picked up the tray and backed towards the door. He barely gave Carradine a second glance as the other rose lazily to his feet, moved slowly across the small room towards the bureau near the door. One hand holding the tray, the guard nodded, swung the door with the other hand, releasing his hold on the handle as he did so. Out of the corner of his eye, Carradine saw the man turn his back as he moved away from the door and out into the corridor. The door was already closing. Acting swiftly, instinctively, knowing that if the guard turned even for a single moment, everything would be lost, he slid the slender metal strip between the door and the jamb. There was a faint grating click, sufficiently like the closing and locking of the door for it to be mistaken for it. But the door was not locked. The metal strip had successfully prevented it from closing properly and the lock had not gone fully home. Slowly, Carradine let the breath go from his lungs, realised that he had been holding it from the moment the guard had stepped out of the room with the tray. So far, so good. Now he would have to wait and pray that no one would think of visiting him until he was ready to make his next move. He checked the watch on his wrist. It was a little after eight o'clock. There was almost an hour to go before Vozdashevsky left his room and made his way to the office along the tunnel.

Carradine felt the seconds and minutes begin to drag. Once he stepped through that door, everything would have to go with military precision. He would need all of the luck in the world — and then some. A lot was going to depend on the guard and Vozdashevsky keeping to their usual schedule. It only needed the Lieutenant-General to depart from it by a minute and it could mean failure.

Watching the second hand of the watch sweep relentlessly around the circular face, he dug the nails of his fingers into his palms. Inwardly, he thought: We knew that the Russians were good, but nobody knew they were quite as good as this. He could understand his chief's concern, knew there had been no exaggeration when the other had stated, quite simply, that millions of pounds had been poured into South America over the past few years. It would have cost millions to build these vast underground chambers, quite part from the instrumentation.

At precisely ten minutes to nine, he checked the knife along his wrist, put out the light in his room and opened the door quietly. For a moment, it had refused to budge and he had experienced a skin-crawling tickle across his chest as it seemed to him that he had failed at the very beginning. Then the door had swung open, the strip of metal falling into his hand. A quick glance up and down the passage and he was outside. Carradine tensed. The dull, monotonous sound of machinery was still audible, something which never ceased. There would be men working all through the night here, working against time to get everything completed on schedule.

He reached the end of the corridor, turned left and walked quickly in the direction of the main tunnel. In the glare of the powerful lights, everything stood out starkly and clearly. It needed only one man to enter the tunnel and he would be seen. As he approached the bend some fifty yards ahead of him, where the gleaming rails curved out of sight before stretching straight up to the surface, he slowed his pace a little. Somewhere just around the bend, the guard should be pacing back and forth in front of that door set in the solid rock. Carradine tightened the muscles of his body, pressing himself close in to the smooth concrete wall, placing one foot carefully in front of the other. The slightest sound now could bring a warning shout, perhaps a bullet. His pulse was racing, his heart hammering in his chest, thudding painfully against his ribs. A faint breath of wind sighed along the tunnel, touched his face. Sweat lay in a cold film on his forehead and limbs.

A few moments later, he peered cautiously around the curve of the tunnel. The guard was there just where he expected him to be. Breathing slowly in an effort to lessen the tension within him, he paused for a moment, watching the man as he paced up and down, just to one side of the rails. The other was one of Donovsky's security men, a simple-minded man from the expression of his face, a man who carried out his orders exactly, who never deviated from his rhythmic pendulum-like movement. Carradine had been relying on this. An Englishman placed on guard might have stopped every now and then unexpectedly, perhaps to glance behind him as he marched, or to take a short breather when he knew no one to be watching him. Had that been the case, the chances of discovery were high. But with a man like this, animal-like and unimaginative, the danger was that much less.

Carradine eyed the shadowed opening of the passage leading to the storeroom, less than fifteen feet from where he stood, waited until the guard had reached the point nearest to him. A second later, the man had turned, was striding away, his back to him. Noiselessly, Carradine ran along the side of the tunnel, measuring the distance with his eyes, planning each step he took. A quick sideways leap and he was inside the passage before the guard had reached the far end of his stretch.

Carradine slowly relaxed, checked his watch. It was four minutes to nine! There had been no noise to warn the guard. Gently, he slid the long-bladed knife from its slim leather sheath. It glinted bluely in the faint light in the passage. Carefully, he wiped the palms of his hands on his trousers, then waited as the seconds slowly ticked themselves away into a vast eternity.

The sound of footsteps coming along the tunnel jerked him abruptly upright, the tip of the knife blade was cold and hard between the finger and thumb of his right hand. Vozdashevsky would be armed, he knew that; but the knife was not intended for the Lieutenant-General, but for the guard. He would have to be killed in the split second after Vozdashevsky opened the door. Once that was done, the die would be cast and he would be forced to see this thing through to its conclusion, one way or the other. With a dead guard on the site, they would soon know who he was and what his purpose was.

The tall, mountainous shadow moved across the passage as Vozdashevsky stepped past along the tunnel. He did not pause to glance along it and was still walking towards the door and the pacing guard as Carradine edged towards the entrance, stood poised, his right arm hanging loosely and relaxed by his side. Slowly, inch by inch, he moved his body forward. Vozdashevsky had paused outside the door of the office. He held a bulky file under one arm and there was a bunch of keys in his other hand. Carradine heard him say something in a low undertone to the guard. Then he had found the key he wanted, inserted it into the lock. The guard had his back to Carradine as Vozdashevsky turned the key, pushed open the door. Carradine drew back his arm until the wrist was level with his neck, then swung it forward at a blurring speed. The knife flashed across the intervening space. The guard uttered a low cough, collapsed to his knees, the rifle falling with a clatter on to the floor of the tunnel. In the doorway of the office, Vozdashevsky turned abruptly, dropped the keys from his hand and fumbled for the pistol at his waist. He was seconds too late.

Before he could unbutton the polished leather flap of the holster, Carradine had reached the doorway, leaping forward in the final spring, one hand to the man's throat, the other to the gun. Vozdashevsky went backward as the other's weight thudded into him, knocking him off his feet. The bone-shaking impact emptied the Russian's lungs of air with a harsh grunt. His arm flailed, papers from the file spilling over the floor of the office just inside the door. There was no time to think out any moves, every second was precious now. His fingers found the carotid artery, squeezed with all of the strength in his hands. Vozdashevsky writhed and struggled ineffectually on the floor, legs threshing wildly, lungs labouring for breath. He was virtually unconscious now, but some animal instinct made him struggle on as he attempted to throw Carradine off. Savagely, Carradine pinned him to the ground with his legs. The Russian's face purpled as he continued to increase the pressure. Somehow, the man succeeded in dragging the pistol from its holster. Air whistling in and out of his tightly-clenched teeth, he brought it up, trying to point the muzzle at Carradine's chest, his arm wavering with the tremendous effort he was exerting. Lifting himself a little, still thrusting down with his powerful fingers, Carradine shifted his body a little to one side, then dropped his knees on Vozdashevsky's right arm. There was a sickening crack as the bone snapped with the force of the blow. Throwing all of his weight forward now, Carradine saw the other's tongue protrude from between his lips, the eyes flicker up until only the whites showed. Then it was over. Lieutenant-General Vozdashevsky, one of the most powerful men outside of Russia, was dead. Gasping for air, Carradine got to his feet, moved out into the brightly-lit tunnel, grasped the guard by the legs and hauled him in through the doorway. He returned for the other's rifle, then closed the door softly, stepped over the crumpled body of Vozdashexsky and switched on the light. The safe stood on the far side of the room. It was a formidable looking piece of metal, he thought tautly, possibly wired to give an alarm if anyone tried to break into it.

Bending in front of it, he checked the exterior carefully, nodded to himself as he located the thin wire which led from the back into the wall. It was the work of a moment to cut it. Fifteen minutes at the most! The thought pounded incessantly through Carradine's skull as he went to work on the safe. Very soon, the guard would be missed. At any moment, someone could come along that tunnel outside and initiate a chain of reaction which could result in his discovery.

Danger could be felt in this room. It crowded in on him from all sides. The sweat popped out on his forehead and trickled down into his eyes so that he was forced to keep brushing it away with the sleeve of his jacket. The tumblers began to drop, one by one, deep within the heavy metal shell of the safe. He gave a faint sigh, then held his breath, as he listened carefully to them. With the proper equipment he could probably have opened this safe within a couple of minutes. It was a type he knew, one he had come up against in the past. But working only with his sensitive fingers and his ears, it was a longer job than he had anticipated.

He glanced at his watch once more. Ten of the fifteen minutes he had allowed himself were already gone. Deliberately, he sharpened his senses. Five more minutes and he would have to leave, try to make for the plane, whether he got the papers from the safe or not. His prime objective was to stay alive and get word of that submarine, carrying its highly lethal cargo, through to Washington. Once that was done, there might be the opportunity of giving the whereabouts of this secret site to the authorities and letting them take whatever action they thought appropriate in the circumstances.

The last tumbler fell into place inside the locking mechanism of the safe. Carefully, he tugged at the heavy metal door. It opened ponderously on thick, oiled hinges. The muscles of his jaw clenched at what he saw inside. On the top shelf were stacks of notes, roubles, pesos, American dollars and some Bank of England five and ten pound notes. There must have been a small fortune there, he reckoned. What could all this be needed for? To bribe officials, to smooth the way for the building of this site, as well as to pay the workmen and scientists there? Every man, they said, had his price. There was enough here to satisfy all but the most avaricious of men.

He ignored the money, turned his attention instead to the papers stacked neatly on the lower shelf. He riffled quickly through them. The vast majority were in Russian and he scanned them rapidly. Reports from Moscow demanding information of a technical nature on the progress of the work. Secret despatches. Three books of codes which alone would be worth their weight in gold to London or Washington. He thrust them into his jacket. Straightening, he took a quick glance around the office. The faint sound just beyond the door reached him a moment later. He did not move. His senses seemed to sharpen themselves like those of a hunted animal's. Then he moved quickly, stepped towards the door and switched off the light. In the darkness, every sound seemed to become magnified. Holding his breath, he strained every sense. There was nothing. The faintly humming pulse of the machinery in the distance was still there, still unchanged. Had he been mistaken? Somehow, he did not think so, but certainly that faint sound had not been repeated. He pressed his ear close to the thick metal door. Silence. He stood up, straighter. Something set his spine tingling, heightened the tension in his body.

Gently, he twisted the handle of the door, opened it a crack. A thin strip of light shone through into the room, fell on the upturned features of Vozdashevsky a few feet away, on the tongue which lolled stupidly from the open mouth and the wide, sightless eyes that seemed to stare in the dimness as if the man was still alive, looking at him with an accusing glance. With an effort, he thrust the idea out of his mind, opened the door further and glanced out. The tunnel stretched away on either side of him, empty and silent. He let his breath go in a series of slight whispers. Stepping out into the tunnel, he closed the door behind him, held one arm tightly across his jacket where the code books now reposed, pressing in to his chest.

Now to get up to the surface, out into the open, and make for the plane. He did not doubt his ability to fly it once he got behind the controls. Had it been one of these new-fangled jets, there might have been some difficulty, but not with a DC-3. A further quick check of the tunnel behind him, leading down into the depths of the hillside, then he turned and began to walk quickly in the other direction.

The sudden sound behind him was a blend of a fierce hiss and a dull plop. In almost the same instant, there was a shrill whine as a bullet struck the ground near his feet, certainly within an inch of his right shoe, and went ricocheting along the tunnel.

Carradine stopped at once, knew this was a trap, and that he had somehow walked right into it. Slowly, with no expression whatever on his face, he turned his head and looked behind him. Ten yards away, three men stepped out into the tunnel. Donovsky held the pistol almost carelessly in his right hand, a thin wisp of smoke lifting from the barrel, the smooth bulge of the silencer clearly visible where it had been screwed on to the end. The two men at his back were soldiers. They held their rifles rock steady, the round holes of the muzzles pointed straight at the pit of his stomach.

Letting his arms hang loosely by his sides, Carradine flexed the fingers, held himself taut. He wondered if they would shoot him down there and then, or whether they would wait until they had questioned him. The latter seemed more likely. He felt the dryness in his mouth as he tried to swallow. There must have been a second warning alarm in that room which he had overlooked, an alarm which had sent out its warning to these men, had brought them hurrying to the office, waiting for him to step out into the tunnel where they could take him with the least amount of trouble.

He felt a feeling of anger at himself run through him. Donovsky walked right up to him, motioned the two men towards the closed door of the office, barking a sharp command as he did so. They opened the door and stepped inside, switching on the light.

'Somehow, Senor Perez — if that is your name — I had thought you would be sufficiently intelligent to take my earlier warnings seriously.' The narrowed eyes did not flicker. 'For this you are going to die, but there will first be some questions to answer. We have ways of getting the truth out of you, should you decide not to co-operate with us.'

7

The Tortures of the Damned

A moment later, there was a sudden yell from inside the room. The dead bodies of Vozdashevsky and the guard had been discovered, together with the open safe. Donovsky whirled instinctively. He would have been less than human not to have done and Carradine's actions were automatic. He knew that he could not hope to finish these three men, that by now the alarm would have been spread throughout the whole length and breadth of the site. It would be out of the question, even if he got away from these three, to reach the waiting plane.

Taking a quick step forward, he swung with his straightened hand. The side of the palm struck Donovsky hard on the wrist, almost breaking the bone. The gun clattered from his nerveless fingers and the momentum of the blow rocked him back on his heels. Donovsky shouted fiercely at the top of his voice. Savagely, Carradine hit him across the adam's apple, but the other was turning away at the same moment and the blow did not have the paralysing force it would normally have carried. Swiftly, he tried to turn the other, saw the man's face glistening with sweat, heard the clatter of running feet as the two soldiers burst out of the room.

Then the roof of the tunnel seemed to fall on him from a tremendous height. Something struck him with a sudden stunning force on the nape of the neck. His hand reached down to try to grab at Donovsky's tunic, then kept on going, his body pitching after it. He was unconscious before he hit the floor, did not feel the impact as he fell at Donovsky's feet, hands still curled as he sought to grab the other and pull him down with him.

How long he was unconscious, he did not know. The first conscious impression he had was of a whirling, shining haze of light somewhere at the back of his eyes and a hammering pain in his skull which seemed to beat in time to the thudding of his heart. Cautiously, he opened his eyes, then squeezed them tightly shut again as light, stronger and sharper than that which beat in his brain, sent a stab of red agony searing through into his forehead. His stomach heaved, brought a wave of sickness into his chest. There was the taste of vomit in his mouth. He tried to swallow, to force it away, and failed. Slowly, carefully he managed to control his breathing. That was the first step towards clearing his brain. Gradually, he was able to think properly. Gingerly, he opened his eyes the merest fraction of an inch. The harsh, glaring light was still there, shining directly on to his face, but this time, he was able to keep his eyes open and to focus them on the object. It seemed to be suspended over his upturned face, so close to him that he could distinctly feel the heat from the powerful bulb.

Carefully, he tried to move his hands and legs but they refused to obey him. For a second, the thought came to him that he had been partly paralysed by a blow to some part of the body. Then he realised that he had been strapped down by his wrists and ankles so that it was almost impossible to move an inch.

'Now, Senor Perez,' said a voice which he dimly recognised, 'we can begin with the questioning. There is much that I wish to know and I feel quite sure that you are going to tell me everything.'

'What makes you think that there is anything to tell?' Carradine spoke through lips strangely swollen. He tried to turn his head, to shield his eyes against the powerful glare of the light, but his head seemed to be held in some way.

'Come now, you must take me for a fool. You carefully plan things so that your door does not lock properly this evening, you then hide yourself in the passage leading to the storeroom and wait for the Lieutenant-General to arrive. After killing both him and the guard you open the safe and steal some extremely important papers. There is only one conclusion I can draw from that. What did you intend to do with those papers if you had succeeded in getting away from here?

Who is your contact? Where is he now?'

'I intended to sell them to the highest bidder.' Carradine tried to infuse some measure of conviction into his voice.

'I see.' The other's tone sounded almost bored. 'That is not a very satisfactory answer. All of this was planned, and planned very carefully. For you to get here, you had to pass our agents in Montevideo and they are not easily duped. Yet your papers, your background, were all checked, and found to be impeccable. Again, there is only one explanation. I do not believe you are speaking the truth. I do not believe that you are the man you represent yourself to be and consequently, there must be a very large and well-organised group behind you, who have provided you with a fake background which was sufficiently authentic and far-reaching to fool us.'

'And what have you gathered from that?'

The other ignored the interruption, went on quietly. 'With an organisation of that size and ability behind you, I consider you are working either for the

American or the British Secret Service.'

With an effort. Carradine gave a harsh laugh. 'If you care to think that, then you are quite at liberty to do so. But if it were true. I would get nothing whatever out of this. I reckoned those papers in that safe were worth at least ten, maybe twenty thousand pesos.'

Donovsky shook his head slowly. He said in a quiet, well-modulated voice: 'I'm afraid that you still do not understand. Whatever you have managed to discover about our work here, which I suspect may perhaps embarrass us, will be of no use whatever to you now. There is no way for you to communicate with your contact outside. Very soon, we shall dispose of you and your death will not be very pleasant I assure you.'

'I can imagine that,' said Carradine grimly. He tried to ease his tortured body into a more comfortable position, but with the straps binding his wrists and ankles effectively, it was impossible to do so. He let his muscles relax. There was one thing in his favour. These men did not know his true identity. So long as he was able to keep that information from them, there was a slender chance that something might be salvaged from the ruins of his mission. Although he might not be able to see it through to its completion, when it became obvious that there would be no report from him, someone else might be able to pick up the threads back in Montevideo. There was Merton's death which the FBI must surely be following up. One of their top agents could not just die like that without someone being detailed to look into it and whatever else might be said about them, when it came to having one of their men killed, they were not fools.

Whether they would find out anything in time was a debatable point. He closed his eyes, tried to think clearly. A sudden sharp pain on the top of his skull forced him to open them wide again. He sucked air in through his parted teeth, heard it whistle down his throat. The tight-fisted grasp had almost pulled his hair out by the roots, bringing tears to his eyes. The harsh light wavered in front of his vision.

'You still have not answered my

questions.' The calm, inexorable voice penetrated the wall of pain around him. 'As I said, we have ways of making you talk, and ways of knowing whether you are telling us the truth. It will be very unwise of you to go on lying to me.'

The man behind him twisted his fingers, jerked his head around so that the agony in his neck was almost unbearable. Fire tore along his muscles. He fought for control. Sweat trickled down his cheeks, dripped off his chin. The pull on his head increased. Through his tear-blurred vision, he saw Donovsky's face peering at him through the shimmering glare. The other smiled, drawing back his lips over his teeth.

'This is all so very distressing,' Donovsky said softly. 'I personally do not like to have to use these measures. But you force me to do so. Now, who are you? What is your real name? Who are you working for?'

'My name is Perez. You know that already. Why persist in trying to find something when there *is* nothing else?' Carradine spoke through tightly-clenched teeth. A questing finger reached down the side of his neck, sought for a particular nerve and then applied a gently increasing pressure. The sweat broke out afresh on his face, ran into his eyes. More pain. More sweat. More questions. How long would this go on before he broke down, told everything, just so that the body-searing agony might stop, even for a moment?

Desperately, he tried to pull himself upright, fought against the bonds which held him down. It was useless even to attempt to move. The pressure on his throat increased momentarily. Fire burned its way along the nerves down one side of his body. A thin, high-pitched scream forced its way through his lips and after that, he knew nothing for a long time.

★   ★   ★

When he regained consciousness a second time, it was darkness which had taken the place of the glaring, actinic light. He opened his eyes with an effort, held them open, felt the blackness push down against his eyeballs like a huge piece of velvet. Was it really dark here, or was he blind? Panic went through him for a second. Swiftly, he fought it down. He found that he could move his hands and legs now. Somehow, he sat up, then swung his legs to the floor and stood up. The blood rushed pounding sickly to his head and he swayed, would have fallen again had not his outstretched hand struck the wall nearby. With a tremendous effort, he remained on his feet, shaking in his arms and legs. Where was he? What had they done with him after he had lost consciousness?

Blindly, he groped forward, touching various objects without being able to recognise them. Gingerly, he felt his way around the wall of the room until his fingers probed around the edge of the door. There ought to be a light switch somewhere on the wall close by, he told himself. Running the palm of his hands over the smooth wall, he located it a moment later, pressed it down. Light flooded the room and the quick look around hurt his head. He was dazzled by the light, unable to see clearly for a long moment. Then he saw that he was back in his quarters. He went over to the long iron bed and sank down on it with a sigh. Sweat had pooled on his body and his clothing was sticking to his skin, chafing it painfully with every movement he made. He felt as if he had been pummelled and beaten all over, yet there were no bruises on his flesh. That man who had carried out the punishment at Donovsky's command had known his job. He had, in all probability, been specially imported for this one task. His talents would only be required on certain occasions, but when they were needed, he would apply all of the dread knowledge which the Russians had built up in the years since the Revolution, combining the worst of the Gestapo and the Japanese Kempe Tai in their methods.

He felt a shiver go through him as he sat and stared about him, still dazed by what had happened. Clearly they have placed him here to recover from his ordeal until they were ready for him again. Unconscious or half dead, he was of no use to the torturer. It was essential that he should have all of his wits about him, should be able to feel pain. Was there any way in which he could kill himself before the next period of torture came? A sudden thought came to him and he got to his feet, moved slowly to the bureau. Opening the topmost drawer, he reached for his shaving kit. That at least would provide him with one way out. He found himself staring down at the empty drawer, only vaguely comprehending.

He went back to the bed and stretched his aching body out on it. He did not know how long he was going to be given to recover. But he needed time in which to think. In spite of his intention to think things out, he felt asleep almost at once. The next thing he knew, there was a slight touch of cold wind on his face, and he was awake almost at once. Even before he opened his eyes, he knew that the door of the room had been opened and that one of the guards was standing there. He feigned sleep, but it was no use. The other came forward and prodded him roughly on the shoulder.

Turning over on to his side, he opened his eyes, looked blankly at the other. The man's face bore no trace of expression. His rifle was slung over his shoulder but he kept well back from the bed, evidently taking no chances with this man who had already killed two men on the site and who might still be dangerous.

The guard pointed towards the bureau with a quick motion of his hand. Screwing up his eyes, Carradine forced himself into a sitting position on the bed. His skull threatened to split open and for a moment dizziness swept through him. He saw the tray which had been left for him, nodded his head with a conscious effort, and watched the man go out. This time, the other checked that the door was securely locked.

Realising that he was both hungry and thirsty, Carradine staggered across the room. As he reached the bureau, a wave of sickness went through him and he had to clutch at the side of the drawers to steady himself. Sweat lay cold on his forehead as the spasm worked its way through him. Conquering the sudden dizziness, he straightened up, swallowed, then glanced down at the food in front of him. There was a bowl of thick soup, two slices of bread and a mug of steaming coffee. He chewed the food slowly and mechanically, swallowing at intervals. His mind was beginning to function again. Evidently Donovsky meant to keep him alive for the time being. Possibly he had some other fate in store for him, rather than starving him.

Seating himself on the edge of one of the chairs, he sipped the scalding coffee. Whatever happened, he must have upset the smooth running of this place by what he had done. He wondered how Donovsky would explain to his superiors, the death of Lieutenant-General Vozda-shevsky and the guard, the fact that one of the employees here had been able to get into that office and the carefully locked safe. Donovsky would be a very worried man at that moment, he thought with a touch of grim amusement. His report to Moscow would take a lot of writing and it was extremely doubtful if he would be able to satisfy his superiors in his section of the M.G.B. All of this would combine to force the other to any lengths to get what information he could from Carradine. Perhaps, in that way, he might be able to justify himself in the eyes of the men in Moscow.

The guard returned for the empty tray fifteen minutes later, then left. Carradine sat back. He longed for a cigarette, but all of them had been taken from him. Acting on impulse, he checked his pockets. Empty, every one of them. His shoes, however, had not been touched. One was empty, the knife blade which had been concealed there having been lost some-time during the past few hours. But the other was still intact. He listened at the locked door for a moment, then sat down on the chair and unscrewed the heel from the shoe. The small, but sharp blade nestled snugly in the palm of his hand, the finely-tempered steel gleaming in the light. With this, he still had a chance, he thought. But how to use it to its best advantage? Donovsky had decreed that he was to stay alive for the time being.

Therefore it meant there would be more questioning to come. Before that happened, he would have to act. Kill the guard when he next came with food? The man would be doubly alert now and for all Carradine knew, there could have been a second man standing out there in the passage in case he made any move like that.

His mind raced around details of a handful of pitifully desperate plans, assessing and rejecting them almost at once. None offered him any hope of success. It was as if he had had his chance, and having failed, fate had decreed that he would never get another. His head ached and the mere act of thinking made it worse.

The beating he had received had been too much for him. His only chance was to sleep on it and trust that something would come to him once his mind was capable of thinking more clearly and precisely. Everything in him warned him that there was not time for that, that every second wasted could mean the difference between success and failure. In the end, however, commonsense prevailed and he lay back on the bed, closed his eyes, and surrendered himself to sleep.

He woke with a start, the light from the lamp near the ceiling shining down into his eyes. Lifting his arm, he brought the watch on his wrist close to his face and peered down at it. Almost ten o'clock. Night or morning? he wondered. Down here in the bowels of the earth, there was no way of telling. He blinked, sat up, rubbed a hand over his forehead, wiping the faint sheen of perspiration away. What was going on outside that door which shut him off from the outside world? Were they discussing how to get rid of him? Had they already decided what his fate was to be.

A little while later, the door opened abruptly, without any warning. A guard stepped in, followed a second later, by Donovsky. Carradine watched the other's face closely as the man came forward, seated himself without a word on one of the chairs facing him.

The other looked searchingly at him for a long moment, then said in a pleasant tone: 'I have been informing Moscow of developments here. They are extremely perturbed at the turn of events, particularly the death of Lieutenant-General Vozdashevsky.'

'I thought they would be.' Carradine said softly.

The cold eyes narrowed a little but beyond that, the other gave no indication that he had heard a word Carradine had said. 'They have given me certain instructions which I shall see are carried out. Fortunately what has happened has not interfered with our work here. Nevertheless, it is obvious, both to them and to me that you will have to be eliminated. Naturally, they wish to have any information they can get. Accordingly, I am prepared to offer you a choice. Tell me everything I want to know. And I will personally ensure that your death is both quick and painless. Refuse, and you will scream for death to come and release you from your agony.' His tone was suddenly businesslike. 'Now, which is it to be? The choice is yours.'

'If there was anything to tell, I would

have told you.' Carradine said sharply. 'I assure you I don't like the way your man tried to break every bone in my body.'

'That is exaggerating things a little, but it was nothing to what he can do given the opportunity. It is very seldom that he had to exert himself. Even the most stubborn people talk before that stage is reached. I would advise you to think over very carefully what I have said. In — ' he consulted the watch on his wrist as he spoke ' — an hour's time, you will be brought for further questioning. During this period of reflection, I trust that you will go over these things and reach the right decision.'

'Surely you don't think that you can get away with killing me,' Carradine said tightly. 'There will be others looking for me and once they find my body, they will get on to you and this little scheme of yours will be blown sky-high.'

Donovsky's smile broadened. 'I'm sorry to have to disappoint you. But unlike the others who attempted to run away from here, I mean to ensure that your body will never be discovered. You seem to have found out quite a lot about our plans. Since you know so much, knowing a little more can do no harm, and it may serve to show you how futile any effort on your part will be. One of our submarines is bringing the nuclear warheads from Russia. It will stand off the coast in twenty-four hours from now and the cargo will be brought ashore and then transported here in a small fleet of trucks which we have for the purpose. When the submarine leaves again, it will have one additional passenger. Whether you are killed here or on board the submarine is of no material consequence. Once dead, your body will be fired through one of the torpedo tubes.' He ran the tip of his forefinger down the side of his face, his voice amiable. 'Perhaps you have never seen a human body once it had been subjected to the action of such pressure. I assure you that it is not pleasant. Your remains will be deposited somewhere on the floor of the Pacific and that will be the end of it.'

Carradine tried to repress the shiver than went through him. What a way to die, if he was doing to die. And the trouble was, that most of this was due entirely to his own stupidity, through trying to do too much. Instead of trying to get his hands on those papers and code books, he should have made straight for the plane. That way, at least, he would have been able to warn the FBI of the Russian submarine which was bringing in those warheads.

Donovsky got easily to his feet. He stood for a moment looking down at Carradine. His lips curled into a faintly sneering smile. 'Whoever you are,' he said thinly, 'you made a big mistake when you tried to fight us. We are too big an organisation for you. Your only hope now is to be sensible and choose the quickest death.' Turning sharply on his heel, he went out. The guard closed the door behind him.

An hour. That was all the time he had. Somehow, he had to think out that plan he needed so desperately. No matter how slender the chance, he would have to take it, for once they got him back in that ghastly room with the blazing arc light shining down into his face, all hope would be gone, lost irrevocably. His mind spun. There was only one chance left to him. It would all depend on how many men Donovsky sent to fetch him when the time came for more questioning, more interrogation. By now, the other may have decided that there was nothing more to fear from him; that now they recognised the danger, they could deal with him quite easily. If that was so, if Donovsky sent only the one guard to take him from this cell, this pitifully thin plan of his might conceivably work.

He settled himself down to wait. The slender knife nestled in the palm of his right hand. At least he still had this. It had not been discovered in the process of searching him for concealed weapons. That was a start anyway.

Thirty minutes. Forty-five. It seemed the longest hour that Carradine had known in the whole of his life. Evidently, Donovsky intended he should have the full sixty minutes in which to ponder his fate and make his decision. The other must surely have known what it would be when he had offered him that alternative, yet he was playing this game out to the full. Possibly they were trying a war of nerves with him, hoping that he might break under the strain.

Exactly on the dot, the handle of the door rattled. As it swung open, he got slowly to his feet, stood in the middle of the room, waiting. The guard stood there, the rifle at the ready. He motioned Carradine to move out of the room, stood well to one side of the door as the other moved forward. With an effort, he concealed the feeling of relief as he noticed that the corridor was empty except for this one man. So Donovsky was now absolutely sure of himself. The guard thrust him forward with a sharp movement of his hand, swung the door shut behind him. Without moving his arm, Carradine eased the blade into position in his palm, gripping it tightly with his curled fingers. Now the other was beside him, motioning him along the corridor in the direction of the main tunnel which lay some thirty yards ahead.

Carradine moved reluctantly, hanging

back. The guard swung impatiently towards him, lips thinned, one arm lifted towards the butt of the rifle. His face was twisted into a grimace of angry warning. But the sideways movement had swung the man off balance. Only slightly so, but it was enough for Carradine. In a sudden savage motion, he swung the knife, brought it arcing down on the other's back, just on top of the lungs. His knuckles struck the rough cloth of the man's uniform as the knife blade went in all the way, driving down through the flesh with all of his strength behind it. A ghastly sucking moan came from the man's lips. For a second he remained on his feet, arms swaying, pawing at the air in front of his contorted face as if trying to grab something invisible which hung there. Before he could fall, Carradine had caught him around the middle, lowering the body to the ground. Apart from that brief bleating gasp for air, there had been no sound. Quickly now, he thought tensely; get out of here and up to the surface before Donovsky became tired of waiting and realised that something was wrong. Panting through clenched teeth, he ran swiftly for the end of the corridor. A small diesel locomotive, hauling a couple of trucks, moved smoothly along the tunnel. He glimpsed the man at the controls as the train moved past him. Then it was gone and he was sprinting along the tunnel, the breath rasping in his throat, lungs heaving with the strain. There was the best part of a quarter of a mile to go, and all of it uphill. Long before he had covered that distance, his legs were on fire with the tremendous exertion. Several times, he half fell and only succeeded in keeping his balance by a desperate grab at the side of the tunnel. The light glared in his eyes, light from the overhead lamps, from the glittering metal which lined the tunnel on both sides, from the rails which stretched all the way to the surface.

There was no sound from behind him. How long he would have before there was any pursuit, he did not know. In front of him, the upward slope ceased. The bright lights were all behind him. There was the smell of the jungle in his nostrils and the cold rush of air in his face. Staggering as he ran forward, he reached the end of the tunnel and collapsed into the wet undergrowth that grew thickly in front of him.

It was night, a dark night with no trace of a moon and any stars which might have been visible were completely hidden from view by the thick canopy of leaves and branches which formed an impenetrable blanket over his head. He lay quite still, unable to do anything while the breath gushed in and out of his lungs and the sweat on his body sent a shivering spasm through his limbs. Then he forced himself to his feet. Cautiously, he made his way through the jungle, moving the small branches and creepers out of his way, taking care to make no more noise than was necessary.

The trees thinned. Soon he would be out of the jungle and on the edge of that vast area which had been cleared, bulldozed flat. Thrusting himself through a wall of vine, he almost pitched down the steep slope in front of him. In the faint shimmering of starlight, he was just able to make out the contours of the ground. Six inches from his feet, it dropped for perhaps ten feet, then continued smooth and level all the way to the long, concrete building perhaps a quarter of a smile away, a dark shadow that thrust itself up from the artificial, man-made plain. Just beyond it and a little to one side, he made out the silhouette of the DC-3. At least it was still there. During that long, heart-breaking run through the tunnel, he had been haunted by the fear that it might have gone.

The stretch of ground between the jungle and the control block was a heap of tumbled rocks and huge boulders. Evidently the bulldozers had pushed most of the surface roughness out here when they had cleared the airstrip itself. Now these same rocks afforded him the cover and protection he needed. For all he knew, there were still guards watching the airfields and the buildings here, even though the initial scare had faded.

He paused instinctively as he came within sight of one of the small wooden buildings nearer at hand. The squat shape loomed up at him from the dimness almost without warning and he crouched low in a small hollow as he scanned the area carefully. At first, he could make out nothing, but his instinct told him there was danger here and it was a feeling he had never ignored in the past. With his knees bent under him, he turned his head slowly, then paused abruptly. A faint orange spark had appeared briefly near one of the huts. It was gone as he swung back and tried to pick it out again, but he felt sure that he had not been mistaken. It was the glow which might have come from the tip of a cigarette as a man drew deeply on it. Cautiously, Carradine lifted his head and surveyed the area around the hut once more. He felt a tiny prickle of sweat on his forehead.

The orange pinpoint of light showed once more and this time he fixed its position accurately, knew exactly where the man was standing. Now why had they posted a guard on that particular hut? Because it housed something of vital importance? It was not large enough to hold any of the complex equipment. If it had been any other piece of machinery, surely they would have kept it underground, instead of out here.

Then what else was there? His brow furrowed in thought for a moment as he turned the various possibilities over in his mind. When it finally came to him, he cursed himself silently for not having thought of it before. That German rocket expert who had been kidnapped from Montevideo — Gunther Henkel. It seemed likely that he had refused to co-operate with these people and they were keeping him prisoner here until he changed his mind. He recalled that he had not seen Henkel down below, although he had seen a photograph of him back in London and would have recognised him instantly if he had come face to face with him. None of the other men had mentioned him by name either. It was as if he did not exist here.

Carradine turned the thought over in his mind. This meant that he might be able to alter his plans a little if he could get Henkel out of there, and if the other could fly that plane. Cautiously, he edged his way through the rocks, placing his feet carefully so as to make no sound. He approached the small hut from the rear, out of sight of the guard. A gust of cold wind sighed around the corner of the wooden building. He heard the sound of the guard's boots on the rocky ground as the other shifted position. It would be cold work standing guard during the night, he mused. No wonder the other had risked punishment to smoke a cigarette.

He still held the knife which had killed the other guard in his hand. Instinct had enabled him to run and forget all about it, while still retaining a grip on the weapon.

Risking a quick glance around the corner of the building, he made out the shadowy figure of the guard less than five feet away. The man was staring directly in front of him, the cigarette dangling from his lips, one hand on the rifle slung over his shoulder, the high collar of the greatcoat he was wearing turned up around his neck against the cold. He looked uncomfortable, evidently wishing his turn of duty was over and he could get next to some warm radiator.

He was round the corner of the hut and on the other before the man was even aware of his presence there. The other swung back, mouth opening to yell a futile warning, one hand clawing desperately for the rifle, fear written all over his face as he realised that death was very close. Almost automatically, Carradine kicked out with his left foot, the toe of his shoe catching the other just inside the knee, knocking his legs from under him. As he went down, his left hand swung at the man's neck, caught him with a sickening thud just behind the ear, the force of the blow almost lifting the guard clean off his feet, hurling him against the wooden wall of the hut. His scream died in his throat before it could reach his lips. His head jerked back on his neck like that of a puppet, or a marionette with the controlling strings suddenly snapped. It was a deadly blow which could have killed instantly had there been just a little more savage force behind it. As it was, the man lay slumped against the base of the wall, unconscious, and likely to remain that way for a very long time. Carradine stared down at the knife held between the fingers of his other hand, then thrust it into his pocket. Murder was sufficient when there was no other alternative. He did not wish to kill this man who now represented no danger to him. Donovsky might do that when he learned how the guard had allowed himself to be taken by surprise at his post.

The door of the hut was locked, but Carradine put his shoulder to it, thrusting at it with all of his weight. The lock held the first time he tried, but the second blow snapped the lock with a faint screeching of metal and the door fell in with an abruptness that almost sent him off balance. He recovered instantly, went inside cautiously. His voice was a low whisper as he called:

'Henkel! Are you in here?'

'*Ja!*' There was surprise in the low voice which came from the far corner of the room. 'But I do not understand. Who are you and how did you know I was here?'

Carradine caught the other by the arm

as the man moved forward. 'There's no time to explain things now. We have to move fast,' he said tersely. 'The guard is unconscious, but at any moment, others might come once they find I've escaped from down there.' He jerked a thumb in the direction of the tunnel. The other nodded his head quickly to show that he understood.

'They tried to make me work down there, helping them to build this secret site. When I refused they locked me in here, kept me without food in an attempt to break me.'

'You'll be able to explain all of that later,' Carradine said, his voice rough and urgent. 'At the moment, I have to try to get you away from here. Can you pilot a plane?'

'I'm not sure.' The other's voice expressed surprise. 'They brought me here in a plane. I used to fly before the war, but that is nearly thirty years ago.'

'Do you think you can remember enough to get that plane off the ground and fly it to Montevideo?' Carradine saw a shadow cross his eyes. Then the other stiffened with a sudden resolve. 'If that is the only way we can get out of here, then I'll do it, of course. But why can't you fly it?'

'Because I won't be going with you. Now hurry. Once you're in the air the rest is up to you. They won't be able to follow you from here. It's the only aircraft on the site.'

'I understand,' nodded the other. By now, they were standing almost directly beneath the wing of the DC-3. 'But what about you.'

Carradine caught the other by the arm, his fingers biting into the other's flesh urgently. 'Listen to me,' he said tightly. 'There is a Russian submarine coming to rendezvous with these people sometime tomorrow night. I don't know where or when it will be. But it's carrying several nuclear warheads for these missiles on board. I want you to get word through to the authorities in Washington. Tell them that Carradine gave you this information. They can check with British Secret Service headquarters in London if they need confirmation of this. Whatever happens, they must stop that submarine from landing those atomic devices. I think you can understand the consequences if they succeed.'

The German nodded his head hurriedly. 'I can visualise what would happen,' he affirmed grimly. He threw an apprehensive glance at the plane, the mass of cold metal that loomed over them. If he felt any doubts as to his ability to fly it, he gave no verbal expression of them, but merely said quickly. 'Why must you stay behind, Carradine. What is there for you to do here?'

'Just in case you don't make it. I have to follow them to their point of rendezvous, try to do something myself. It's the only way of finding out just where they propose to meet. I may be able to direct any planes to the area if you get word through in time. Now get up there and get this crate off the ground. With luck, you should make Montevideo before dawn.'

He half pushed the other forward, watched tensely as the German climbed towards the cockpit. He tried not to think of the odds that were stacked against them, of how many things could go wrong during the next few hours. If Henkel did succeed in getting this plane off the ground safely, it might hold one tremendous advantage for him. The Russians would almost certainly jump to the conclusion that he was in that plane with Henkel. It would give him more scope during the hours of daylight which would be the most dangerous as far as he was concerned.

Three minutes later, the starboard engine started up with a spluttering cough that sent the echoes booming from the distant rocks, chasing themselves among the trees. The propeller began to spin, slowly at first, then more rapidly, whirring into an invisible blur. Black smoke streamed momentarily from the exhausts. Then the port engine fired and Carradine was deafened by the noise. He moved back until he stood in the shadows of the control block. The plane shuddered as Henkel fed more power to the motors. God, would everything go all right. Or would Fate step in once again and wreck all of their hopes? He knew how Henkel must be feeling at that moment, seated behind that glittering array of controls, possibly far more complex than any he had known in the years before the war when they had flown nothing more advanced than the slow-moving biplanes, aircraft with the minimum of controls. Slowly, the DC-3 began to trundle forward. It began to turn into the wind. The roar of the engines beat at Carradine's ears as he turned and began to run towards the high rocks on the very edge of the clearing. If Donovsky needed any further indication of where he had got to, the sound of the DC-3 taking off would provide him with it.

Crouching down behind the cover of the huge, misshapen boulders, he saw the plane hesitate as it reached the far end of the runway. Then it began to roll forward, increasing speed as it did so. Just keep it nice and level until you've got enough speed to lift the nose clear of the ground, thought Carradine, through tightly gritted teeth. He found himself almost willing the plane off the ground and safely into the air. Fortunately there was no crosswind, otherwise it might have been impossible. As it was, Henkel just made it, with scant yards to spare. The under-carriage of the aircraft cleared the tops of the trees on the very edge of the runway by less than six feet. Then it was climbing steadily into the dark night sky, the throbbing thunder of the engines fading slowly into silence.

He let his breath go in a loud exhalation. God, but that had been a close thing. Henkel was not out of the wood yet. He still had to fly that plane all the way across Argentina to Montevideo. But as he had discovered himself when it came to piloting a plane, getting it off the ground and down again at the other end in one piece were the difficult things. The bit in between was relatively simple. Unless the other ran into a storm such as they had encountered on their way there.

Cautiously, he pressed himself close to the hard ground as a group of men came running out into the open from the direction of the jungle.

8

The Big Gamble

Inwardly, Carradine felt oddly pleased with himself. Although his body ached and the heat had brought the sweat out on his limbs and face, he was now in a position where he could look down on the whole of the site below him and watch every bit of activity that went on. He was too far away, to identify any of the men he saw with any degree of certainty, but it became apparent as the day went on, that Donovsky considered he had left with Henkel, and also that they were still determined to go through with their original plan of picking up the nuclear warheads from the coast. Indeed, Carradine would have been very surprised if things had gone otherwise. It meant that they would have to take extra precautions, but their plans were now so advanced that it would have proved

269

impossible for Donovsky, already labouring under the heavy responsibility of Vozdashevsky's death and Carradine's escape, to cancel their meeting with the submarine. By now, he reckoned it would be somewhere in international waters, some miles off the coast. It would remain there, submerged, until dark, when it would move in closer to land, ready to meet the boats which would put out to it and take off the warheads.

Shortly before noon, five trucks had been driven out into the open. They must have been kept underground, ready for work such as this. He would have given anything for a pair of powerful binoculars so that he might keep a closer watch on things. Several men busied themselves around the trucks during the early part of the hot, sultry afternoon, tinkering with the engines, checking wheels and tyres. They could not afford to have a puncture on the road to the coast and back, not with a cargo like this on board the vehicles.

Winding his watch, he wriggled his body into a more comfortable position.

The heat was energy-sapping. It lay like a thick, tangible blanket over everything and dehydrated him. His lips and throat were parched and it was painful to swallow. Below him, the ground shimmered and shook in the heat haze and an occasional flash of bright sunlight, reflected from some metal piece of one of the trucks would burn across his vision. He felt sleepy and everything conspired to make him sleep. The heat, the damp smell of the jungle around him, looming at his back where it lifted up the slope of the hill in a thick green blanket, the dull ache which was suffused throughout his body, the fact that he had not slept properly for almost twenty-four hours. Unconsciousness was not sleep and did not bring rest or refreshment, he now discovered. He screwed up his eyes and forced them open again. He could not afford to go to sleep. He would have to keep a close watch on those trucks down there, judge the moment when the men were ready to move out and get down there and into one of them without being seen. The fact that no one suspected he was still there would help him, but it might not be enough of an advantage.

He carefully lifted his arm. Almost three o'clock. He doubted if the trucks would begin to move until it was almost dark, but he could not afford to take the chance of relying on this. He closed his mind to everything but the need to stay awake no matter what happened. There was too much at stake for him to make another mistake. He had made too many already. A lot depended on Henkel, and if he failed in his attempt, then still more depended on him. He could hitch a ride on one of the trucks and with any luck at all, reach the destination with these men. But what then? There was no chance of destroying the submarine himself. If he could somehow wreck the trucks with the warheads on board. He concentrated on that thought, though at the moment he could not see any way of doing it. But at least, it served to keep him awake.

Two hours later, he spotted the small group of men making their way up the steep slope just beyond the place where he knew the entrance to the main tunnel to lie, hidden in the fringe of jungle. His gaze followed them until they disappeared into the dense foliage. Had they been sent to scour the jungle for him? Was Donovsky still not certain that he had gone on board that plane? He raised his head very carefully an inch at a time, estimating the route those men were likely to take. If they were to swing round once they got into the really dense jungle, they would come out somewhere close to his hiding place. He forced his body to relax.

He could not be sure they were looking for him. They could have been sent on some quite innocent errand utterly unconnected with him. But he could not afford to take unnecessary chances. Keeping an eye on the clearing below him, he shifted his position. It meant that his view of the ground below was somewhat obstructed, but it was the best he could do in the circumstances.

Dusk was a rapid darkening of the sky over the jungle. It came with an unaccustomed swiftness, surging in from the east in a rush of purple which blotted out the reds and golds on the western horizon. The sun had dropped over the rim of the world like a penny going into a black box. Carefully, Carradine moved his stiff body. His circulation was sluggish. He tried to rub his limbs to bring some of the feeling back into them. Very soon, there would be some renewed activity down there and it would be time for him to move and make his play. The darkness was almost complete when he noticed the men beginning to file out into the wide clearing. His heart jumped, hammering into the base of his throat as he began to make his way down through the rocks, moving as quickly as he dared. One wrong move and he might start a minor avalanche of rocks which would give the game away at once.

In the darkness, he was able to approach to within twenty feet of the line of trucks, keeping his body low. The men were getting on board the vehicles now, two men inside every cabin except the very first. Carradine recognised Donovsky, as the other clambered up beside the driver. So the Head of Security would be travelling with them. He nodded to himself in the darkness, threw a swift, all-encompassing glance in every direction, then darted forward, leapt for the top of the tailgate of the rear truck. His fingers caught at it, clung there for a moment. With a wrenching of shoulder muscles, he hauled himself up into the back of the truck. The canvas fell back into place, hiding him from prying eyes.

He settled himself in as comfortable a position as possible, heard the engine start up a moment later. Then the truck was rolling forward into the darkness, bound for its meeting on the coast.

★ ★ ★

For more than an hour, as near as Steve Carradine was able to judge, there was no sound but the muffled roar of the engine as the line of trucks filed on through the night, following a winding, tortuous route to the west. The metalwork creaked continually. Time and again, he was flung from one side of the truck to the other as they swung sharply around the twisting

275

bends of the road. Obviously this road was seldom used. Soon, they would be on their way down to the sea. Then there was a lot to be done. He could not hope to tackle all of these men, but if he was able to get one of them alone, separated from the others, he might be able to grab his uniform, giving himself the chance of mingling with the others.

Then he would have to play things as they came. If Henkel managed to get through to Washington and convince them of the truth of what he said, there might be a welcome interruption. If not, it would be up to him to try to do something.

With a sharp jerk, the truck began to slow. He felt his muscles tense as he crouched close to the tailgate. The truck swung suddenly, almost threw him off balance. Desperately he hung on to the metalwork. They had driven off the road now. Bumping and heaving, the truck moved forward, swaying precariously from side to side as they hit patches of uneven ground. Lifting the canvas, he peered out into the darkness that lay all about him. At first, he could see nothing. There was a dull muted roaring in his ears which could be heard even above the sound of the engines, but for a long moment he was unable to recognise it. Not until the truck turned sharply once more and he was able to look out over the smooth expanse of sand that lay to one side, did he realise that it had been the booming of surf on the beach.

Without pausing to think, he pulled himself over the lip of the high tailgate, paused for a moment on the edge, then dropped to the ground. He hit hard, bent his legs as he struck the ground, flexing the muscles of his knees and thighs, rolling over to break the force of his fall. No sign from the trucks, now drawing to a halt in the near distance that anyone had heard him. Scuttling towards the line of rocks nearby, he flung himself down on the wet sand behind them, panting through clenched teeth. For the moment, he was safe. But what now? The moon was beginning to rise. He could just see it over the rising black hump of the land behind him. Very soon, it would be light enough to see by and that could increase the danger to him.

He saw the men climbing down from the trucks. There were no lights visible and he guessed that Donovsky did not want to advertise their presence there until he was ready to signal out to sea where the submarine would be moving towards this part of the coast, looking for their signal.

There would be a little while to wait yet, he reflected. Donovsky would be sure to get there with plenty of time to spare. He too had made his share of mistakes during the past few days and he would not want to run the risk of making any more. The moon laid a distant shimmer on the water, yet for some strange reason, Carradine noticed that the land seemed brighter than the sea. Maybe it was just an optical illusion. The thought went out of his mind at that moment. One of the soldiers had moved away from the line of trucks, was heading towards the rocks near to where Carradine lay. He did not pause to guess at the man's purpose, knew only that this was the opportunity he had been waiting for. He moved his body slowly and carefully, got his legs under him, the muscles bunched, ready for the upward and forward leap.

Carradine had no illusions as to what he had to do. There would be no giving this man a chance to live. He would have to be killed, instantly and without any noise. The first upward stab of the knife in his hand would have to be utterly decisive.

The dark shadow came forward, picking its way carefully through the sharp rocks, careful where he put his feet. There was no sound except for the dull, monotonous booming of the surf and an occasional voice from the men near the trucks. The knife was cold and hard in Carradine's right hand. He held himself ready as the distance between the man and himself decreased. The other was only five yards away now, still unsuspecting. He felt his muscles tighten under his flesh. If only one of the men at the trucks glanced round at the wrong moment, it would be the end. But it was a chance he had to take, a calculated risk as Merton would have described it.

The man's face was in profile as he stepped over the rocks, half-turned away from where Carradine was hidden. Almost lazily, the other lifted himself to his feet, moved forward like a wraith. The knife flashed for a second before it struck downward, buried itself to the hilt in the man's back. The other uttered a little cough, half-swung to face his attacker, mouth dropping slackly open, eyes widening in that last, despairing moment before death came. He went down on to his knees, wavering backward a little, arms struggling to lock themselves around Carradine's thighs, to pull him down with him in his death throes. The fingers gripping his trousers suddenly loosened, fell away. The man arched his body backward into an impossible posture. Then with a slithering motion, he fell back, his head striking the rocks with a sickening crunch that sent a little tremor along Carradine's spine.

Without pausing, he thrust the knife into his belt, bent and stripped the heavy greatcoat off the dead man, shrugged into it, thrust the shapeless cap on top of his head and hauled the rifle free of the man's shoulder, looping his own arm through the sling.

The job was done. In the darkness, he should pass well enough for one of the soldiers and his knowledge of Russian would ensure that he did not slip up when any orders were given. He felt reasonably sure that nobody would find the dead man among the rocks.

Donovsky had moved forward now, away from the line of trucks, down to the water's edge. He was standing with his hands clasped behind his back, like some present-day Napoleon looking out over the battlefield at Waterloo. A moment later, he turned and called something to one of the men. The other walked forward and the two men spoke together in low voices, occasionlly pointing out to sea where the gentle swell brought the waves lapping over the smooth, sandy beach.

Out of the corner of his eye, Carradine noticed the cruel, pointed rocks which rose up for perhaps twenty feet on either side of this short strip of smooth sand.

Donovsky had certainly known what he was about when he had chosen this spot for their rendezvous.

It was a weird scene. The dark shadows of the trucks drawn up in an almost mathematically straight line on the beach. The men gathered about them, and those two figures outlined against the moonlit water, everything in absolute stillness. Something would have to happen to break the strange spell which seemed to hold everything immobile.

Donovsky came back, walking slowly, the other man trailing close behind him. He stood in front of them and spoke quietly: 'The submarine is due to arrive within ten minutes. I want each of you to keep a sharp look-out. You all know what to do when the time comes.'

The men nodded slowly. Inwardly, Carradine felt a growing sense of defeat. He was here, but there seemed nothing he could do. How could one man prevent what was sure to happen here within the next few minutes? He glanced at the rest of the men on either side of him. Try to hold them up with the rifle he had slung over his shoulder? The idea was so ludicrous that it would have been laughable had the situation not been so serious. He racked his brains for some idea, no matter how fantastic, no matter if it meant giving up his own life, if he could prevent those nuclear warheads being landed and taken back to that launching site. He looked past Donovsky, out to the flat, oddly featureless expanse of the sea where it stretched away to a seemingly limitless horizon. Nothing whatever broke that smoothness. Maybe the submarine had been unable to reach this place; he rejected the thought as soon as it crossed his mind. That was nothing more than wishful thinking on his part. Whatever he did it would have to be something more positive than that.

A sudden shout from one of the men jerked his head around. He narrowed his eyes as he stared in the direction of the man's pointing finger. His breath caught at the back of his throat. The smooth, sleek and unmistakable shape of a submarine, surfacing from the ocean depths, was clearly visible against the horizon, the moonlight gleaming faintly off the polished metal hull.

Donovsky took charge at once, snapping orders to the men with a machine-gun speed. Everything on the beach went with military precision, each man knowing what was expected of him. Donovsky himself had moved back to the water's edge, holding the heavy signalling lamp in his left hand while he flashed the coded signal out to sea.

Desperately, Carradine looked about him for some sign that Henkel had got through and a trap had been laid. There was nothing. No MTB boat out there to take care of the submarine. What sort of international complications might occur if that happened? Possibly even if Henkel had done his tuff and informed Washington of what had happened, even if they had checked the story with London and knew he was telling the truth, they would decide they could do nothing.

That was one possibility he had wondered about while he had been lying up there on the fringe of the jungle, with the tropical sun beating down on the back of his neck, but he had tried not to consider this possible, had bolstered up his courage and endurance with the thought that whatever happened, the suffering, Merton's death, and Henkel's courage, would count for something in the long run. Now, it seemed, his first thoughts on the subject had been close to the truth. Washington either could, or would, do nothing. He was on his own now and his position was growing more precarious with every passing minute. Very soon now, the submarine would move in closer once they had verified the signals they were receiving and the boat which he had seen being loaded on to the first truck, would go out to meet them. Then the transfer would take place, the submarine would go back to Russia, the nuclear warheads would be taken to that well concealed place in the jungle, and the balance of power would abruptly swing away from the NATO Alliance in this important area of the world.

Wearily, he lifted his head, almost as if looking for some sign from heaven that his efforts had not all been in vain. He expected nothing. His mind scarcely registered the fact that there *was* something there. It almost passed unnoticed before he swung his gaze back once more, narrowing his eyes to make it out more clearly. The moonlight had glinted briefly on something high in the sky to the west. He felt sure he had not been mistaken. There it was again.

Now, he could just make out the faint drone of heavy and powerful engines. The bomber came in on a long run, gliding down over the sea. When it was almost directly over the spot where the submarine lay, something tumbled from the belly of the plane. Carradine felt the pupils of his eyes contract painfully as the flare burst. The expanding sphere of actinic brilliance lit everything on the sea and threw long shadows around the group on the beach, picking out details clearly.

Donovsky was yelling something at the top of his voice, waving his arms wildly as he ran back across the beach. Carradine gripped his rifle more tightly as the men began to scatter and run for the trucks.

Overhead, there was the powerful, synchronised clamour of the engines as the bomber swung around in a tight circle. Then it was heading in again and this time there was a deadly purpose behind its approach which Carradine could sense a few moments before the depth charges tumbled from the bomb bays of the plane and splashed into the water in a pattern around the submarine. He felt the muscles of his stomach tighten convulsively as he waited for the inevitable explosions. They came as a series of muffled, oddly faint thuds. Then the sea around the submarine suddenly erupted in a ring of waterspouts that lifted high above the deck. Tons of water cascaded down on it, hiding it temporarily from view. When he could see again, the bow was lifted clear out of the water at an incredible angle. It was impossible to see whether any damage had been done, but it seemed incredible that such titanic underwater explosions could have hammered against that hull without cracking it like an eggshell in places.

As if in answer to the questions that

were running through his mind at that
moment, the bows lifted even higher until
they were pointed directly at the star-
strewn heavens. Then, slowly and
smoothly, the Russian submarine slid
down beneath the waves and vanished
from sight.

As the plane roared overhead like some
vengeful angel of doom, Carradine was
aware that Donovsky was yelling fiercely
at him from the cab of the leading truck.
Quite suddenly, he realised that he was
the only one standing there, that all of the
others had climbed back into the trucks
and the engines were revving up fiercely.
He waved an arm to indicate that he had
understood, turned as if to run towards
the last truck in the line, waited until he
was hidden by its bulk from the eyes of
anyone who might be watching and dived
for the cover of the rocks. At any
moment, he expected to hear a shout
from one of the vehicles, now beginning
to turn and move off in the direction of
the main road. But no sound came and
less than five minutes later, there was
silence on the lonely stretch of beach,

silence except for the fading thunder of the bomber as it headed back in the direction from which it had come. Of the submarine, there was no trace. Not even the oil slick which usually discoloured the surface of the sea whenever one was sunk. It had undoubtedly gone to the bottom, taking with it the nuclear warheads which had been destined for the missiles at the launching site. Somehow, he had the feeling that the Reds would hesitate before they sent any more now that they were aware that the Americans knew of the presence of the launching site on their very doorsteps.

★   ★   ★

Ten days and several thousand miles later, Carradine thrust his long body back in the chair in front of the polished desk, his hands resting loosely in his lap.

'So they managed to sink that submarine after all,' said the man behind the desk musingly. The sharp eyes rested on Carradine's face for a long moment, then the other leaned back and lit a cigarette, watching the blue smoke curl lazily towards the ceiling. Outside the window, the roar of London's busy traffic could just be heard in the distance. 'I think we can take it that the launching site will lose much of its military significance now that its presence and position is know to the world at large. As for our friend Donovsky, it wouldn't surprise me greatly if he isn't in Russia at this moment, having been recalled to explain his conduct.'

'I certainly wouldn't like to be in his shoes right now, sir,' said Carradine with a faint smile.

'The usual treatment,' nodded the Chief. He flicked the ash carefully from the end of his cigarette. 'They do not treat failures with kid gloves as we are inclined to do over here. Sometimes, I think that is why they make such deadly opponents. When a man is eternally facing a death sentence, he makes sure that every mistake is made by the other side. Perhaps I am being a little too lenient in this respect.'

'In what way, sir?' inquired Carradine softly.

'Well, let us consider your own particular case, Carradine. Your orders were to locate Gunther Henkel and the means by which the nuclear warheads were to be smuggled into South America. They included nothing about stealing these people's secret code books and thereby placing yourself and the success of your entire mission in jeopardy.'

'In the circumstances, there seemed nothing else I could do, sir.' It was a lame excuse, as far as the Chief was concerned, but it was the best he could contrive. 'I am sure that the South American Governments will be only too pleased to co-operate with us now that this has been brought into the open in this way.'

'In the event, everything seemed to have turned out remarkably well.' The Chief paused, looked mildly across at Carradine, resting one hand on the top of the desk. 'I suppose you will be looking for a spot of leave after this little episode?'

'Well, it wouldn't come amiss, sir,' Carradine answered.

'Very well.' The Chief gave a brief nod. 'But be careful. It may interest you to know that Donovsky had been tipped off about you almost from the beginning, by a woman. Could it have been Valentina Veronova?' There was an almost cherubic smile on his face as he spoke.

THE END

We do hope that you have enjoyed reading this large print book.

Did you know that all of our titles are available for purchase?

We publish a wide range of high quality large print books including:
Romances, Mysteries, Classics
General Fiction
Non Fiction and Westerns

Special interest titles available in large print are:
The Little Oxford Dictionary
Music Book, Song Book
Hymn Book, Service Book

Also available from us courtesy of Oxford University Press:
Young Readers' Dictionary
(large print edition)
Young Readers' Thesaurus
(large print edition)

For further information or a free brochure, please contact us at:
Ulverscroft Large Print Books Ltd.,
The Green, Bradgate Road, Anstey,
Leicester, LE7 7FU, England.
Tel: (00 44) **0116 236 4325**
Fax: (00 44) **0116 234 0205**

Other titles in the
Linford Mystery Library:

THAT INFERNAL TRIANGLE

Mark Ashton

An aeroplane goes down in the notorious Bermuda Triangle and on board is an Englishman recently heavily insured. The suspicious insurance company calls in Dan Felsen, former RAF pilot turned private investigator. Dan soon runs into trouble, which makes him suspect the infernal triangle is being used as a front for a much more sinister reason for the disappearance. His search for clues leads him to the Bahamas, the Caribbean and into a hurricane before he resolves the mystery.

THE GUILTY WITNESSES

John Newton Chance

Jonathan Blake had become involved in finding out just who had stolen a precious statuette. A gang of amateurs had so clever a plot that they had attracted the attention of a group of international spies, who habitually used amateurs as guide dogs to secret places of treasure and other things. Then, of course, the amateurs were disposed of. Jonathan Blake found himself being shot at because the guide dogs had lost their way . . .

THIS SIDE OF HELL

Robert Charles

Corporal David Canning buried his best friend below the burning African sand. Then he was alone, with a bullet-sprayed ambulance containing five seriously injured men and one hysterical nurse in his care. He faced heat, dust, thirst and hunger; and somewhere in the area roamed almost two hundred blood-crazed tribesmen led by a white mercenary with his own desperate reasons for catching up with the sole survivors of the massacre. But Canning vowed that he would win through to safety.

HEAVY IRON

Basil Copper

In this action-packed adventure, Mike Faraday, the laconic L.A. private investigator, stumbles by accident into one of his most bizarre and lethal cases when he is asked to collect a fifty thousand dollar debt by wealthy club owner, Manny Richter. Instead, Mike becomes involved in a murderous web of death, crime and corruption until the solution is revealed in the most unexpected manner.

ICE IN THE SUN

Douglas Enefer

It seemed like the simplest of assignments when the Princess Petra di Maurentis flew into London from her island in the sun — but anything private eye Dale Shand takes on invariably turns out to be vastly different from what it seems. Like the alluring Princess herself, whose only character flaw is a tendency to steal anything not actually nailed to the floor. Dale is in it deep, mixed-up with the most colourful bunch of fakes even he has ever run up against . . .